Wack City

Welcome to the Real Las Vegas

Miko Montgomery

Mimar Publications

WACK CITY: WELCOME TO THE REAL LAS VEGAS

Second Edition 2025

First edition published in 2022 under the title
Wack City: Tales of the Real Las Vegas.

ISBN 979-8-9879334-1-1

Cover design © 2025 by Miko Montgomery

Printed in the United States of America

For information about this and other works,
visit: www.mikomontgomery.com

Mimar

Publications

This book is dedicated to my Mom who said I should be a writer. The book is also dedicated to the legions of unknown Hollywood writers who were ripped off and kicked to the curb.

Contents

Acknowledgments

I'd like to thank John L. Smith, Jeff Rice, Jeff McBride, Tom Bleecker, Lillian Strange, and Clive Barker. I'd also like to give a special shout out to all the Vegas OGs who opened my eyes to the truth.

Book cover concept/design by Miko Montgomery

Introduction

I moved to Las Vegas in the fall of 1999. There was still a lot of boom in the town at that time. The local economy was robust and the city seemed to offer endless opportunities.

Las Vegas was a magnet for people looking to reinvent themselves with a little help from Lady Luck, and they came from all over the world. I hit the ground running. I immediately got a job at a local music store, played solo musical gigs on the weekend, and did video production work. Later, I even opened my own business, a poster store where I also sold books and movies.

Unlike most people moving to Vegas, I didn't bring a lot of preconceived notions. Las Vegas is mythic, and I understand why, but it never held any attraction for me. I had family in the entertainment business who lived in Vegas back in the glory days, back when the town was *really* booming. So, I was certainly aware of it, and connected to it, but I never found it compelling. Las Vegas always seemed *square*. I come from a family of jazz musicians, so my idea of cool is Miles

Davis, not the Rat Pack. Even the iconic Las Vegas Strip seemed goofy and cartoonish.

Las Vegas has always promoted itself as being Sin City, a label it wears with great pride. "What happens in Vegas stays in Vegas" is the most successful ad campaign in the history of the city. Yet once again, I found Vegas lacking. Compared to other cities around the world, Vegas even seemed low on the decadence scale, promising far more than it actually delivered. It's not exactly Babylon. Suffice it to say that for me, Las Vegas was big of tit, small of brain, and way overhyped.

However, within the very first months of my move, I realized that I had been mistaken about Las Vegas. Wildly mistaken. The Las Vegas that's hyped to the world by the tourist bureau is a neon *façade*. The casino experience, showroom entertainment, ultra bars, strip clubs, buffets and other famous Vegas fare are all quite real. However, these things actually serve to *conceal* a reality. The *real* Las Vegas is quite different. The real Las Vegas is characterized by an *occult* truth so startling, few people would even believe it.

I discovered this truth accidentally, by way of the residents I encountered on my various jobs, particularly the older residents. By far, the absolute coolest thing about Las Vegas are the older residents. I've known OGs from all over the world, but they're different in Las Vegas. Vegas OGs are usually colorful, well lived and highly expressive whether they were in the entertainment field or not. But they also tend to have a thoughtful, insightful, contemplative side that caught me by surprise. They are not shallow people. These OGs shattered my belief that Las Vegas was stupid. The more I learned from them, the more I understood just how wrong I'd been.

Ironically, I went from having no interest in Las Vegas to becoming *obsessed*. I bought every Las Vegas book and documentary I could find. I collected newspaper and magazine articles. I even documented my own impressions, maintaining both a Vegas oriented journal and a long running blog. Most importantly, every Las Vegas resident, especially the OGs, became a potential interview subject. When I had my own business, I would routinely invite residents/customers back to my store after hours and conduct videotaped interviews. These interviews proved to be invaluable. Many of them were mind blowing. I was totally unprepared for what appeared to be a general consensus.

What happens in Vegas is *supernatural*.

Eventually, I took everything I had absorbed about Las Vegas over the years and made a short YouTube "mockumentary" called *Occult Las Vegas Revealed*. I considered it a mockumentary because it was a mix of historical facts and creative, sometimes even wild speculation. I initially made it as a response to the aforementioned ad campaign, "What Happens In Vegas Stays In Vegas", a campaign that always annoyed me because of its lack of originality. That slogan is just a slight variation of a similar slogan that's been around for years in sales, sports and entertainment. Not exactly creative, particularly coming from a powerful, massively funded tourist bureau. In addition, the campaign was yet another example of the brainless way in which Las Vegas promotes itself. I knew I could do far better with zero funding. *Occult Las Vegas Revealed* was originally designed to be my own ad campaign for Las Vegas, a creative campaign meant to show the city in a whole new way.

Soon after posting my mockumentary on YouTube, I disabled the "comments" feature. The word *occult* is provocative and tends to freak some people out. So, after being accused of spreading evil, Satanic doctrine, I pulled the plug on all comments. By the way, the word *occult* only means "hidden" and nothing more. Fortunately, there were open-minded viewers who were fascinated by the presentation, and they reached out to me via my website. I've collected scores of emails over the years, and the vast majority of them have one thing in common. Viewers didn't find my speculations particularly wild at all. Quite the contrary. Much like my many OG interview subjects, these viewers related their own, often startling supernatural experiences. Many of them actually seemed relieved for the opportunity to do so. I got the distinct feeling that *Occult Las Vegas Revealed* provided some kind of validation for ideas that would have otherwise been considered batshit crazy.

I've spent over twenty years living and working in Las Vegas. I've studied the city with the fanatical zeal of a scholar/historian. My rabid research ultimately consumed me, much like a drug. Even now, I'm somewhat shocked by my own journey from ambivalence to a kind of full-blown *addiction*. Las Vegas grabbed me by the throat, and it's never let go. But that's Las Vegas. Once you find Las Vegas, Las Vegas finds you.

I wrote *Wack City* as a way to address and perhaps, process the occult truth of Las Vegas, a truth that both excites me and terrifies me.

Welcome to Wack City; where dreams come true, and nightmares too.

Miko Montgomery
Las Vegas, Nevada
2022

Wack City

Welcome to the Real Las Vegas

Welcome to Wack City

Night. A passenger plane cruised over the city of Las Vegas in preparation for descent. Jill Levy sat in her window seat, watching the world-famous Las Vegas Strip glow in the darkness below. The pilot announced that the plane would be landing soon, increasing the level of excitement among the passengers.

Jill was more than ready to land. She had hoped to take a short nap on the one-hour flight from L.A. to Vegas but unfortunately, the plane was filled with passengers who had other ideas. The incessant chatter and laughter ruined what might otherwise have been a pleasant flight.

Jill was chill. Sleep or no sleep, she was glad to be onboard and out of L.A.. Las Vegas was no cure for what was ailing her, but it might be a nice band-aid.

A stewardess passed by, reminding everyone to prepare for landing. Jill complied, checked her watch, and looked down at the Strip again. Now that she was here, she began to have second thoughts about coming. Now, the whole idea seemed so impulsive. It was out of character for her — like gambling, something she rarely did. Yet tonight, that's *exactly* what she was doing. But she had a weird feeling about tonight. And she felt lucky.

* * *

Jill walked out of Terminal 3, carrying a briefcase and wheeling a small suitcase behind her. Dressed in red leather and boots, she turned plenty heads, both for her striking attire and for her bold body language. It was clear from her purposeful stride that she was a player, not a plaything, and that whatever she was into, she was the one calling the shots. She greeted flirtatious eyes dismissively.

The passenger pickup area was unusually congested, even by Vegas standards. Like Jill, tons of other people had flown into town tonight. Maybe they felt lucky, too. As she struggled to maneuver through the multitudes, she again questioned her impulsive decision to come to Las Vegas. Her cellphone rang, and she sighed in exasperation. She already knew who it was.

"Look, I don't have time to talk to you right now, okay?" Suddenly the crowd didn't seem so annoying. "I don't know why I even answered. If you want to talk, wait till I get back Sunday night. Better yet, just wait till Monday morning."

Jill paid no attention to the frantic protestations at the end of the line. She was too focused on the crowd that had begun to grow. She was determined to score a cab before things got even more chaotic.

Using her best airport ninja skills, she navigated her way in between and past the slower members of the herd until she was close to the curb. She immediately spotted a cab heading in her direction. She smiled at her good fortune, waving the cab down. The protestations on the phone had continued.

"Are you still here? I told you, we'll talk later. I don't have time for this. I need to go. Goodbye!"

The taxi pulled up directly in front of Jill. The driver leaped out and hurried around the cab to open the passenger door. As Jill moved toward the cab, a couple appeared from behind her and climbed inside. The driver closed the door for them. As he walked past Jill, he looked at her, shaking his head with insincere sadness. Her eyes followed him back into the taxi, and she continued to watch as it sped away. Unbelievable. She looked around, and there wasn't another cab in sight. Jill again second guessed herself about Vegas.

A limousine was idling at the curb a few feet from Jill. It had been there all along, but she hadn't noticed it. But the driver noticed her. The tinted window on the rear passenger side was lowered halfway.

"Miss, I'd be happy to take you wherever you need to go," the driver said. "You're gonna have a hard time getting a cab tonight."

Jill felt lucky again. Without hesitation, she opened the door of the limo, and climbed in, suitcase and all. As the limo sped away from the mob, she smiled with satisfaction. No doubt about it, the limo was a sign, and it was even better than a taxi.

Jill settled back into her seat. The red leather interior made her smile. A wood-paneled partition separated the passenger area of the limo from the driver. A 12 x12 opening was cut into the partition, covered by a mesh grille. Jill couldn't see the driver, but she could hear him perfectly.

"So, what's up with the taxi cabs tonight, or lack thereof?" She asked.

"Well, there's a major UFC event, half a dozen concerts, Celine is back at Caesar's, the AVN awards, and… oh, yeah… the National Gay Rodeo Association is in town, too. Their opening festivities are tonight."

"Yeah? Well, yippy ki yay."

"It's one of those crazy nights when everything is going on at once. Great for Vegas, bad for you. Where are you staying, anyway?"

"I don't have a room yet. I blew in on a whim. I figured I'd just take a chance and book something once I got here."

"You flew in without a reservation? That might be problematic tonight."

"Crystal, my astrologer, texted me this morning and said I was absolutely going to hit some kind of jackpot this weekend. A *major* jackpot. She's been spot on, especially lately. She said there was no doubt about it, that it's all up in my chart. And she specifically used the word 'jackpot.' So, I thought… jackpot… Las Vegas. I had some frequent flyer miles laying around so here I am. It seemed like a brilliant idea at the time."

Jill's cellphone rang, and she rolled her eyes as she pondered whether or not to answer. Finally, she opened her purse and took out her phone.

"Excuse me," she said to the driver, then directed her wrath toward the party on the end of the line. "You need to stop haunting me, okay? I don't have time for this. If I had wanted to talk to you, I would've stayed in L.A."

The party on the line could faintly be heard protesting. Whatever was said, however, fell on deaf ears.

"Of course, I'm upset!" Jill continued. "Do I sound chill? That was the best writeup we've ever had, and they barely mentioned me at all. Unbelievable." She slipped out of her jacket. "You know what your problem is? You're starting to believe all that bunk your new publicist has been writing about you lately. Now you've got Hollywood Head. You think you're a renegade visionary? Wrong. You're just a cog in the wheel. And it's *my* wheel."

Whatever the response, Jill wasn't having it.

"Yeah, well I know you know. It's time other people knew it, too."

The driver interrupted. "Miss, I've got tons of goodies back there. Please help yourself."

Jill noticed that the small table beside her seat doubled as a refrigerator. She opened the door and found it well stocked. At the sight of alcohol, her mood suddenly brightened.

"Oh, my God. Olde English? Are you serious?" She exclaimed, removing a 40-ounce bottle of malt liquor. She didn't bother to look for a glass. She hoisted the bottle with one experienced hand and took a long drink. "Thanks, man. And right on time, too." She picked up the phone again and her smile vanished. "I can't believe I'm still talking to you. We're done. And don't bother calling me back either, because if I see it's you, I won't answer. Now go away for good. And I mean it this time." Jill ended the call and took another long drink, then rested the bottle between her legs. "I haven't had Olde E. in years. I got my jackpot right here."

"I do aim to please." The driver paused momentarily before continuing. "Miss, I sure didn't mean to eavesdrop. Honestly. But I couldn't help but overhear some of your conversation back there. Are you by chance in the film business?"

"That's what it says on my guild card. Yeah, I'm in the business. I'm a producer. My name's Jill Levy."

"What? Really?" The driver was impressed. "I've got Jill Levy in *my* limo? I think *I'm* the one who hit the jackpot."

"You know who I am?"

"Of course, I know who you are." The driver proudly exclaimed. "You're Jill Levy, Carfax Abbey Productions."

Jill was flattered and smiled—at first. "Well, I'm just the producer. The director does it all by himself."

"Well, I'm a huge fan of your work. Carfax always reminded me of Hammer Films from back in the day. An independent company with great production values and great stories. And just like Hammer, your films never look low budget because they're so well crafted. I love Carfax. I really mean it, too. I'm not just saying it because you're my passenger. It's a real honor to have you in my limo. I can't even believe it."

"Well, I'm impressed that you're impressed. And thank you very much for that recognition. It's nice to get a little— whenever I can get it."

"The pleasure is all mine, that's for sure. Wow, it's so weird to have you for a passenger. Small world. I read that piece in *Variety* just yesterday. Nice."

"You read *Variety?*"

"Sure do. I'm a movie brat!"

Jill frowned as she flashed back on her recent phone conversation. "Well, that article was more about Shane than me. I should be used to it by now. Shane does it all by himself. I keep forgetting that."

"Shane Sloan. He's a fine director."

Jill was quick to clarify. "He's an okay director who's had a boatload of breaks and crazy ass luck. I can't believe the kind of luck that dude has had. Unbelievable."

"He's a visual stylist, that's for sure. His films always have a—"

"Visual stylist?" Jill interrupted with a look of mock surprise. "Really? I'll let you in on a little secret. It ain't Shane who's making his pictures look that good. It's his crew. He's got a crew of geniuses backing him up every step of the way. His DP, cameraman, production designer, right down the line. They've been with him for years. And every single one of them is a virtuoso. Shane works with a team of technical Mozarts. They'd make Kevin Smith look good."

The driver laughed.

"Oh, and I almost forgot the best part. They're all devout Buddhists. Every one of them. So, they're super mellow, hardworking, and devoid of all ambition. Every hack director's wet dream come true. Crazy ass luck. All of it. Unbelievable."

"I take it you're not Buddhist?"

Jill took another drink. "Me? Buddhist? No, I'm bitch. Devout, too." She shook her head as she tried to make sense of the situation. "You know what I think it is… why people are so drawn to Shane? It's that hair. There's just something about white boys with blonde dreads. It's unusual. There's something about that look that just hypnotizes people. Some kind of white Marley, Jamaican Jesus vibe or something. It's weird. Shane's just another dumb blonde."

The driver laughed.

"Well, not dumb. He's shrewd. He's managed his career like a champ, that's for sure. So, he's not dumb, he's just not… heavy. He's light, as in lightweight. That's it. He's not particularly well read. And his knowledge of film is surprisingly limited for a director. I'm an encyclopedia compared to him. But he's ambitious. Definitely ambitious. Nowhere near my level though. Not even close."

"He's known for being efficient. He always brings his pictures in on—"

Jill's anger resurfaced. "Oh, he's efficient, all right. And there's a good reason for it, too. I got the reason right here at the end of my leg. It's my foot. He's efficient because I keep this foot in his ass 24/7 till the picture is finished. I'm the one who built Carfax, and I'm the one who put Shane Sloan on the map. Before me, that chump was shooting gangsta rap videos, trying not to get his ass kicked. He was just another *ain't never been* with big dreams. I made his dreams come true. And speaking of dreams, I'm also the one who assembled that technical dream team who make him look so damn good. Unbelievable."

"They'd make Kevin Smith look good."

"They'd make Tommy Wiseau look good. Carfax has

produced nine pictures so far, and not a flop in the bunch. I developed them all. I found those projects and nurtured every one of them. Carfax has a rep for being story driven. And it's all because of me. I'm a story brat. I know story. That's my gift, and there aren't many people out there who can touch me. At Carfax, nothing gets shot till I say the story is right. I don't care how badass a crew is. If there's no story, there's no picture."

"Story is everything."

Jill took another drink. "When I read that bunk in *Variety*, I didn't know what to do first—cry, puke, or kick Shane's sorry ass. The whole thing just focused on him. Barely mentioned me at all. Jill Levy is the renegade visionary, *not* Shane Sloan. All he's got is blonde dreads and crazy ass luck. I didn't work this hard and come this far to stand in the shadow of some hack. Enough is enough. Now is *my* time."

"You're no Buddhist. You're bitch. Devout, too."

"Think I ain't? And when I get back to L.A., the bitch is kicking some ass. But with different boots than these. Something with a more pointed toe."

"But you two have been together for years. There must have been something keeping you tight all this time."

"Yeah, there was. His cock. He's no hack in the sack. Unfortunately, I do have to give him that."

The driver laughed.

"We just had an anniversary, too. Ten years. You believe that shit? Ten years. Unbelievable. Look, Shane's all right. He likes cats. He bathes on a regular basis. He's not a serial killer, at least as far as I know. More importantly, he knows better than to ever cross me. I just want more recognition for what I've done, that's all. And I've done a lot. I built Carfax Abbey Productions and Shane Sloan too for that matter. I may be a chick, but—"

"You're the man."

"Think I ain't?" Jill's anger subsided just a bit. "Well, from now on, I'll personally make sure that Jill Levy gets higher profile. That's my new resolution and my new mantra, too. Higher profile."

"Higher profile for you would be empowering for all women."

"All women?" Jill laughed. "Nigga, please. The only woman I'm looking to empower is Jill Levy. The rest of these bitches are on their own."

The driver laughed. "Maybe you need to direct. That's the high-profile gig."

"Direct? I already do. The director directs the picture, the producer directs the production. I'm old school. Zanuck style. Back in the day, the producer was the Man, and the director towed the line along with everybody else. And that's how we do it at Carfax today. I'm the captain of that ship, not Blondie Locks." Jill shook her head. "Directors. They all just want to be rock stars, anyway. Tarantino is the poster boy for all this rock star director bunk. Tarantino. He thinks he can write, too, but he can't touch me." Jill laughed. "He can touch Kevin Smith, though. But who can't?"

The driver laughed. "You're a story brat."

"Right? I'm a writer who became a producer by

circumstance. I was forced to become a producer because I demand the one thing that writers will never get in Hollywood. And that's respect. Disrespecting writers is a time-honored tradition in that town. Hollywood actually hates writers. Always has. Did you know that?"

"No."

"It's because without writers, Hollywood wouldn't even exist. It couldn't exist. No writer, no story. No story, no picture. No picture, no Hollywood. No nothing. There's a well-kept secret in Hollywood, maybe even the biggest secret in a town full of them. But I'm telling you. The writer is everything, just like the story is everything. They are kind of linked if you think about it." Jill laughed. "That's called truth. Truth in italics. Bold truth. Of course, nobody likes to hear truth these days, especially in Hollywood."

"That's amazing. I had no idea."

"It's not the kind of thing they talk about on *Entertainment Tonight*. They don't write about it in *Variety*, either. Hollywood hates writers because it needs them so desperately. The same reason men hate women. But most writers are too stupid or too naive or too afraid to understand that. So, they've allowed themselves to be punked by a movie industry that no longer cares about story. More and more, Hollywood is being run by lawyers, accountants, and other assorted suits, most of whom are artistically challenged. What do they know about story? Yet, they're the ones calling the shots and giving notes to writers. Telling the writer how to write the damn story. It's insulting, not to mention insane. And yet writers stand in line for the chance to swing on their nuts. Unbelievable."

"It's sad."

Jill sneered. "Sad? Please. Pathetic is more like it. Hollywood writers are pathetic. They're punks. Not all, just ninety-nine percent. They've consented to their own punkification for whatever reasons. Fame, fortune, chicks, dicks, whatever their bag. And they've all got a jones by the way—alcohol, drugs, food, gambling, sex, religion, whatever. They've all got their crutch. That's how those cripples deal with getting punked for a living. Writing for Hollywood is a sorry ass, soul-sucking gig. Telemarketing is way more respectful. A writer gives birth to a story. Stories are like children. Giving your story to Hollywood is like giving your prepubescent daughter to Charlie Sheen."

The driver laughed.

"And when you do see your story—or your daughter again—you're like, 'Who is *this* bitch?' She's totally unrecognizable. She's Miley Cyrus, turned out and tore up from the floor up. Well, in Hollywood, it's the writer's gig to do just that. To turn out his own children. Some gig, right? Unbelievable."

"I feel like I need a shower."

"Well, you'd better make it hot one, too." Jill shook her head in disgust. "Hollywood writers. Some people will do anything for a living. As for me, I'm a producer. OG style, too. So, I don't pimp my kids, and I don't swing on nuts either. They swing on mine."

"You're the Man."

"Think I ain't?"

"You really are a renegade visionary. And a natural born

writer, too. That's got to be tough in the Hollywood you're describing."

"Look, I've been in this business a long time. Obviously, I understand that filmmaking is a collaborative art form and blah, blah, blah. I know that song. And it's quite true. It *does* take a team to make a picture. No doubt about it. But it doesn't take a team to write a story. Certainly not a good story, that's for sure. It takes a story brat."

"The greatest works in literature were written by one person."

"Right? A singular vision as opposed to something that's been dicked to death by a bunch of corporate knuckleheads with delusions of creativity."

"There's a lot to be said for a singular vision."

"Uh… yeah, like the story might end up making some sense, right? These days, I come out of a theater more confused than entertained. Cluttered narratives, big ass plot holes, cardboard characters, trite dialog. And those are the hits."

The driver laughed.

"You don't get problems like those with a singular vision. You get those problems with a committee. Movies are confused because committees are confused. With a committee, you don't get story, let alone art. Instead, you get a camel when the original idea was a horse. You get sequels, prequels, remakes, reboots, and re-imaginings, whatever *that* is. You sure don't get what I need. I need story."

"Story is everything."

"Story is *everything*," Jill repeated with added emphasis

on the word everything. "And you sure don't have to spend the gross national product of a Third World country to get it either. Contrary to the prevailing propaganda, I don't consider writing to be a collaborative art form at all. I sure don't need any help. Besides, I don't take notes. I give them."

"You know what I think?"

"What's that?"

"You said earlier that now is your time. Well, I think you're more right than you realize. I think now really *is* your time. Your time to fulfill your real destiny once and for all."

Something about the driver's choice of words and the assuredness with which he spoke them compelled Jill to listen.

"Jill Levy is a born writer who became a producer by circumstance," the driver continued. "And it's paid off because now you're in a position to be what you were meant to be all along—a writer. And you won't have to swing on anybody's nuts to do it, either. As a producer, you've been busting your ass to bring everybody else's vision to life. Well, now it's *your* turn. Now is *your* time. Time to *write*. Time to show the world Jill Levy's singular vision. Something tells me that once you do that—once you focus on writing— you'll get that higher profile you're after. And then your destiny *will* be fulfilled. Who knows? Maybe you were destined to come to Vegas tonight just to hear me say that. Maybe hearing me say that is the jackpot your astrologer was talking about. Jackpots come in many forms."

Jill sat in stunned silence. For a few moments, she was unable to speak. The driver's words were both remarkable and true. Hearing this truth spoken to her, and by a stranger no less, was both unnerving and devastating. Much like the Roberta Flack song, the driver killed Jill softly with his song. Jill's tough, streetwise bravado and cynicism evaporated, and her eyes now reflected a child-like innocence and uncertainty. She sighed as she struggled to express herself.

"I want to write!" Jill spoke the words like a declaration. "I *can* write. I'm good. Really good." Jill's voice dropped to a whisper. "But I'm scared."

"Scared? Of what?"

Jill's voice quavered as she revealed her deepest fears to a stranger. "What if working in Hollywood all this time has jinxed me? What if it destroyed whatever writing talent I had to begin with? What if it ruined me creatively? Because you can't write without ideas. And I just… I don't have any ideas." Jill's eyes welled up with tears. "What difference does it make how much money I've got, or how many pictures I've made, if I don't have any ideas? Ideas of my own? I've got hella nerve talking shit about Tarantino and Kevin Smith. They've put their ideas out there. Where are my ideas? I don't have any!"

"Somehow, I doubt that."

Jill struggled to maintain her composure. "You were right. All these years, I've been developing and producing other people's ideas, but never my own. *Never.* So, what have I done? With my life? With my career? What career? Some career! All these years… and for what? What do I have to show for it all? A little bit of fame and fortune? That's what I got for pissing on my talent? I turned *myself* out. I'm no better than a Hollywood writer. I'm worse." Tears streamed down her face. "Ain't that a bitch? I'm the punk. I need to be sucking Kevin Smith's cock. Now isn't my time, it's *his* time." Jill broke down completely and wept.

"Please don't cry, Jill. Please. It's okay." There was a sweet sincerity in the driver's plea. Though they were strangers, he seemed determined to speak as a friend. "That *Variety* article just threw you for a minute, that's all. Means nothing. The way you talked about writing tonight, only a natural born writer talks like that. Only someone with a passion for story talks like that. Or even thinks like that. You're so ready it's ridiculous. You're in full bloom. You know that old saying, 'When the student is ready, the master will appear?' Well, here's a saying for you, and I just made it up, too. When the writer is ready, the *ideas* will appear. Jill Levy is ready to write. Now is your time. Think it ain't?"

Once again, Jill sat in silence. She'd stopped weeping soon after the driver's initial plea. His voice was soothing and calming. She recognized his genuine sense of decency. After twenty some years of living and working in L.A., a decent person stood out like a unicorn in a barnyard.

As Jill wiped away the remnants of her tears, she reflected on the driver's hopeful, inspiring words. Everything he'd said to her tonight had been so spot on. It was as if they'd been friends for years. Jill's therapist had never been so profound. Maybe the driver *was* right. Maybe hearing his message tonight *was* the jackpot. Because Jill felt purged. A lifechanging catharsis had taken place in the back of a limo. The driver was a unicorn, and Jill lucked out. Crystal had been right, after all.

"You're right," Jill said. "I did need to hear that. And I needed to hear it tonight, too. I can't even begin to thank you for…" Jill paused with a realization. "Uh, by the way, what's your name, anyway? I've been running off at the mouth nonstop since you picked me up. I never even gave you a chance to introduce yourself. I'm so rude."

"My name is Reuben, and you're quite welcome."

"Well, nice to meet you, Reuben. Very nice indeed. I really do feel like I hit the jackpot tonight. No one's ever said anything like that to me before. It's like you told me something, the very something I needed to hear. I can't explain it. Thank you for that. I really mean it. Honestly. Thank you, Reuben."

"My pleasure. Look at how far you've come already. Don't worry, you'll get to where you want to be. Maybe even sooner than you think. Destinations are a funny thing. Sometimes we're closer than we even realize. One day, you'll get the idea you're searching for, and you'll know it immediately. In a heartbeat. It'll blow your mind. It'll be… *magic*. And when you find that magic, you won't be able to stop writing."

"Magic. Yeah, that's what I'm looking for, all right." Jill paused as she chose her words. "Something completely original, totally fresh and unique. Yet still familiar enough to be recognized and embraced. Now *that's* magic. An idea like that makes the planets line up. Rockets' red glare, bombs bursting in air. O face." Jill contemplated her own words. "Something we've seen before, yet something we've *never* seen before. That's it."

"Uniquely derivative."

Jill sat up from her seat in excitement. "Exactly. That's it exactly. Damn, Reuben, you're good." She removed a pen and notebook from her purse and jotted down the words *uniquely derivative.* She stared at the words. "Uniquely derivative. Did you coin that yourself?"

"Yep. It's all mine. But you're welcome to it. Take it. It's yours."

"I'll do that. Uniquely derivative. You've not only got a great voice. You've got a way with words, Reuben."

"Thank you. I'm a writer, too."

Jill smiled. "Is that right? Well, I'm not surprised. You're obviously quite literate. I could tell that immediately. What kind of stuff do you write, anyway?

"Different things, but I prefer horror and fantasy. Mainly horror. That's why I'm such a big fan of your work. I still can't believe you're sitting back there right now."

"Oh, I'm here, all right."

"You know, as we were talking, I got a crazy idea. I've got a few connections in town. Good ones, too. I know I could pull some strings, call in a favor or two, and get you a room tonight. A really nice room, too. It might take some time to pull it off, but I can do it. I know I can. I'll get the word out to my people. I'll get you something for sure. Don't you even worry about it. So, what do you say we make a little deal? I'll do something for you if you do something for me."

"And what's that?"

"Like I said, I'm a writer, and I think I'm pretty good, too. I've got big aspirations. I've got a pretty cool idea that's uniquely derivative, at least I think so. So, here's the deal. I'll make sure you get a room tonight if you'll let me pitch my idea to you. What do you think?"

"That's all? You just want to pitch me?"

"I don't know anybody in Hollywood. I'd never get a chance to pitch to a real producer. And here I am with Jill Levy in my car. That's crazy luck. Pitching to you would be a dream come true. That's *my* idea of a jackpot. All I want is the chance to pitch my idea. Even if you don't like it, it's still a big opportunity for me. Your professional feedback would be a jackpot for sure. What do you say?"

"Well, it would be an honor, Reuben. Besides, I love a good story. I'm all ears." She slipped off her boots, removed a small pipe from her purse and fired it up. After an unusually long exhalation that filled the limo with smoke, she settled back in her seat with a glazed-eyed smile. "You mind if I smoke?"

Reuben laughed. "No, not at all."

Jill did her best sexpot impersonation. "Okay, I'm ready for you now. Whip it on me, baby."

Reuben began, and his voice became more serious. "My idea takes place in a familiar place. A very familiar place. One of the most familiar places in the world. Right here in Las Vegas. Not the Vegas everybody knows, but the *real* Las Vegas."

"What do you mean… the *real* Las Vegas?"

"Well, when you think of Las Vegas, what do you think of? The Strip, gambling, vice, neon as far as the eye can see, right?

"Tits and glitz."

"Tits and glitz. Exactly. But what if I told you there was something beyond what you see and what you think you know?"

"I'd be interested."

"The real Las Vegas has an occult truth, a truth very much hidden from view. It's not on billboards or on TV or in the tourist literature. And yet, this hidden truth literally defines Las Vegas."

"Interesting."

"There's a powerful supernatural energy that exists in Las Vegas because it was built by ruthless gangsters using the profits of criminal enterprise. Which means that the city was built with blood money—money literally imprinted with fear, exploitation, violence, and death. Blood money has a powerful energy, and it carries a negative charge."

"Makes sense."

"Since the beginning of time, cultures from all over the world have called the desert holy ground. Prophets, shamans, and other seekers of wisdom have gone into the desert in search of enlightenment. Most religions were born in the desert. It's a divine location with a powerful energy. It would obviously carry a positive charge."

Jill smiled. She always thought Vegas was stupid. Reuben offered an entirely different perspective that was fresh and compelling. "That *is* interesting."

"So, what we've just described is a city of sin built on holy ground. As a result, there's a cataclysmic convergence of powerful energies—the negative and the positive, the profane and the sacred, the dark and the light. They converge on one spot, and the spot is called Las Vegas."

Jill drained the remains of the Olde E. She rested both the empty bottle and the pipe on the seat beside her. She had already written the words "uniquely derivative" in a small notebook. Now she jotted down Reuben's ideas about Vegas in the same book. She wasn't smiling anymore.

Reuben continued. "Imagine. A city of sin built on holy ground. It's amazing, but it's certainly not natural. In fact, the very idea is insane. But that's only the beginning. Because when these two opposite energies converge, they explode. Literally. It's a cosmic collision of opposing spiritual energies. Explosions have fallout, and Las Vegas is saturated with it. The supernatural energy that exists here is the fallout from the blast. I call that fallout the Vegas Vibe."

Jill was now writing at breakneck speed.

"The Vegas Vibe manifests itself in several ways," Reuben continued. "It scrambles the brain, which is why people go nuts when they come here. The vibe is a highly sexual energy, so it works like an aphrodisiac, too. Vegas stays horny for a reason. But the main thing you need to understand about the Vegas Vibe is this—it *intensifies* whatever it touches."

Jill was seated directly opposite the wooden partition dividing her from Reuben, facing it. But Reuben's incredible ideas moved her—literally. There was a red cushioned bench that ran along the dividing partition. Jill gathered her purse and briefcase, then moved over to the bench to be closer to Reuben. She opened her briefcase and removed a notebook and a stack of 8x5 note cards. Now she felt prepared enough to continue the conversation. She rested her head beside the mesh opening.

"Well, what do you think?" Reuben asked. His ideas were remarkable, and he knew it.

Jill paused before answering, collecting her thoughts. Reuben's ideas were indeed remarkable, and she knew it, too. But she wasn't about to let him know that she knew it. Jill Levy—the story brat—had just worked out a plot of her own. "Well, it's pretty wild, Reuben. Las Vegas is iconic, so most people already have a fixed, preconceived concept of the city. And it's nothing like what you're talking about… cosmic collisions and spiritual energies. I don't know. It might be too out there. People might not be willing to go that far. But it's certainly different, that's for sure. But keep on. Don't let me stop you."

"By the way, everyone in Las Vegas isn't human."

"Well, Area 51 is just down the road, right?"

Reuben laughed. "There really is an alien presence here. I'm not talking about little grey dudes with bugeyes and buttheads, although I'm not ruling that out either. I'm just saying that a segment of the Vegas population is definitely not human."

"What do you mean?"

"Las Vegas is a nexus point, a spiritual intersection where opposing energies collide and continually explode. This ongoing blast rips at the very fabric of what we call time and space. These rips are literal openings. As a result, Las Vegas is more than just a city. It's a door. The entire city of Las Vegas is an interdimensional gate. That's why there are so many non-human entities here."

Jill poured Reuben's extraordinary ideas onto the notecards, amazed by the words she'd written. "Las Vegas is an interdimensional gate?"

"That's correct."

"Apparently Vegas is more transient than I realized. That's some good shit, Reuben. You could sell that at the dispensary."

Reuben laughed. "It ain't bunk either, right?"

"It's urban fantasy, science fiction, philosophy, theology. It's all that and more. No one has ever thought of Las Vegas like this. It's remarkable. I've never heard any…" Jill stopped. She was so dazzled by Reuben's ideas that she was gushing without realizing it. She immediately went back into character. "But I don't know, Reuben. It's still kind of New Agey though. The general public is so conventional, especially these days. It's hard to say how they'd even react to something that far out." A thought crossed Jill's mind, and she looked distressed. "Uh… you haven't shared these ideas with anyone, have you?"

"Not a soul. I'm kind of paranoid about sharing my ideas. I've never even done it until now."

Jill was relieved. "Good. I'm a big believer in paranoia. It's very healthy. You can never be too careful these days. There's lots of predators out there. I'd hate to see you get ripped off. So, keep this stuff to yourself. Okay?"

"Okay. Thanks. You're probably right."

"I've been to Vegas plenty of times. I sure never thought it was deep though. Just corny and horny."

"Tits and glitz are among the myriad weapons of mass

distraction that hide an occult truth. The real Las Vegas isn't shallow or superficial at all. Las Vegas is epic—*spiritually* epic. Every bit as epic as Stonehenge, Easter Island, or any of those kinds of places. How could it be otherwise when the two major cross streets are transcendence and damnation? There's not a city in the whole world like Las Vegas."

As Reuben continued his explanations, Jill wrote furiously, repeating transcendence and damnation to herself with a smile.

"I know it's way out. But it's a whole new way of looking at Las Vegas. Vegas is already mythic. I've just expanded the myth. Actually, I've *re-mythologized* Las Vegas. My Las Vegas is the spiritual center of the universe."

"Who would have thought?"

"But this is just the set up. May I continue?"

"I can hardly wait."

"So, what I've just given you thus far is my Las Vegas cosmology."

Jill laughed. "Cosmology? I haven't heard that word since grad school."

"This cosmology forms the foundation for everything that follows. Do you remember *The Twilight Zone*?"

"Don't be silly. It's only the greatest TV show of all time. Rod Serling—now there's a story brat for you."

"Okay. But have you heard of the Theater of the Grand Guignol?

Jill thought for a moment. "Uh… yeah… kind of. I remember reading about it somewhere. They did weird stage plays back in the day?"

"That's right. The Theater of the Grand Guignol was located in Paris. From 1897 to 1963, this little theater was one of the most popular French tourist attractions, every bit as popular as the Eiffel Tower and the Arc de Triomphe. Short plays were staged there, and they were unlike anything ever seen before. Tales of horror and madness. Mind blowing special effects were performed live in full view of the audience. Modern horror films owe a tremendous debt to this theater because that's where modern horror was born."

"So modern horror has a French mother? Mon Dieu."

"My idea isn't a film. It's a television series."

Jill had been writing all along and looked up from her notes, intrigued. "A TV series? That's interesting. But I'm curious, why a series instead of a feature film?"

"Modern Hollywood is a well with no water in it. Look at everything coming out in the last few years. Just like you said—sequels, prequels, remakes, reboots, reinventions, and re-imaginings, whatever *that* is. Everything is refried. And if by some miracle, it's none of those, you can be sure it's a comic book."

"You're preaching to the choir, Reverend Reuben. Amen."

"Anybody looking to blaze a new trail had better look to television. Look at all the big directors, producers, and stars coming to television lately. It's like a mass exodus. Creative, imaginative people are sick of the dumb box that Hollywood has locked itself into. I think what we're witnessing is an artistic renaissance. And television is leading the way."

Jill was amazed by the depth of Reuben's industry savvy and nodded in agreement. "It's so weird you're even bringing this up, Reuben. I've been contemplating a move in that direction for some time now. Television is right where I need to be. I just haven't found the vehicle to get me there. You're absolutely right. Television is the way to go."

"Horror is way more mainstream than it used to be. The success of shows like *The Walking Dead* and *American Horror Story* proved it. It's never been like this before. There's never been a better time to do horror television than right now. Now is the time. So, imagine a horror TV show based in Las Vegas, the *real* Las Vegas, a city pulsating with a supernatural vibration. A city inhabited by entities both human and not. The stories would be short and weird like *The Twilight Zone.* But they'd also be crazy over the top like the Grand Guignol Theater. Bizarre stories of normal people interacting with angels, demons, witches, warlocks, mad magicians, psychotic sex workers, soccer moms, lawyers, and any other abnormal life form you can imagine. Las Vegas is as mad as anything on a Grand Guignol stage. And Las Vegas is absolutely *The Twilight Zone* for real. The story possibilities would be endless. Is that uniquely derivative enough for you?"

Jill stared down at her notes, spellbound. Such is the power of magic, and Reuben's astonishing ideas about Las Vegas were indeed magic. As Jill processed the events of the evening, it all seemed so unreal. Like some crazy, wonderful dream. An unexpected ride in a limousine had changed her life completely. Crystal had been right. Jill had hit the jackpot *for real.* She could barely keep from trembling.

"I didn't put you to sleep back there, did I?"

"No, Reuben. I'm wide awake."

"And you've never heard anything like it before."

"Never." Jill wasn't lying. She repeated the word to herself. "Does the series have a name?"

"Sure does. *Wack City*. It's a play on words. Las Vegas is a mob town, so plenty of people have gotten whacked here. And because of that Vegas Vibe I've just described; the city is absolutely insane. It's wack. Hence the name, *Wack City*.

"Nice. I like it."

"Good. So now you've got the cosmology and the concept. Now it's time for the story, or rather, *stories*. Are you ready?"

Jill removed the cellphone from her purse, put the phone in recording mode, and placed it on the seat beside her. "Oh, I'm ready, all right."

"Back in the day when Bugsy and the boys dreamed up Las Vegas, the idea was to build an oasis in the desert for bad behavior. And that's exactly what Vegas is. But, as many a desert traveler has discovered, an oasis can turn out to be a mirage. In Las Vegas, things are often not what they appear to be."

Headshots of Horror

It was late in the day; one of those gray Vegas days when Mother Nature couldn't decide whether or not to rain. And even if she did make up her mind, with Vegas being Vegas, the downpour might last all of six minutes.

A Nissan minivan headed south on Eastern Avenue. As the vehicle crossed Sunset Avenue, a low flying jet overhead began its descent, bringing more dreamers and schemers anxious to try their luck in Sin City. The minivan continued on its way, crossing Warm Springs and finally turning into the Warm Springs Plaza, a crescent-shaped strip mall filled with a variety of businesses, most of which appeared to be thriving. However, three businesses were closed, all of them right next to one another. The minivan parked in front of one of them.

The driver climbed out first. Connor was young, white, short-haired, and bespectacled. He was conservatively dressed in white shirt, black tie, black pants, and black wing-tipped shoes. He appeared to be Mormon.

A woman climbed out of the passenger seat. Nedra was young and black with a style sense that complemented

Connor. She wore no makeup, and her hair was pulled back into a bun. Her blouse was buttoned up to the neck, and the hem of her skirt fell well below her knees and slightly above her ankles. Her sensible, flat shoes completed an ensemble worthy of the *Watchtower* collection. If she wasn't a Jehovah's Witness, she definitely taught Sunday school.

Connor removed a small, four-wheeled dolly from the back of the minivan, which was crammed with boxes of varying sizes. He made some adjustments to the dolly that enabled it to lengthen well beyond its small size.

After adjusting the dolly, he helped Nedra unload the boxes. Soon, the vehicle was completely emptied, and the dolly was stacked with boxes six feet high. Nedra pulled the dolly as Connor followed behind, cradling the tower of boxes to keep them from toppling. They made their way over to one of the closed businesses and waited by the door. There was no signage, and the windows and door were covered with black paper.

Mother Nature finally made up her mind. It started to rain. A late model Mercedes pulled into the parking lot and parked beside the minivan. An older woman emerged and hurried out of the rain and over to where Connor and Nedra stood waiting. Her name was Gwendolyn. She greeted them, then unlocked the door to the business and held it open as Connor and Nedra wheeled the tower of boxes inside.

The three of them entered an abandoned business. It was difficult to determine exactly what kind of business it had been. On the walls were many photographs of people—all faces. They weren't the faces of celebrities or models, but ordinary people. They ranged in size from the very small to poster size. All were framed and hung with taste and care. Perhaps the place had been a gallery of some kind. In a corner were several pieces of furniture—a leather couch, a couple of matching chairs, and a coffee table. There were a few old magazines on the table. It looked to have once been a waiting area. In an opposite corner sat a small pyramid of boxes, sealed with tape. Whatever the business had been, it hadn't been successful and looked to have been closed for some time. The room was blanketed with dust, and thick, unruly cobwebs hung from the ceiling, covering everything in sight.

Gwendolyn closed and locked the door behind them, plunging the store into near darkness. "The light doesn't work in here, so be careful. Follow me and watch your step."

The couple followed after Gwendolyn, with Nedra pulling the dolly as Connor pushed from behind. Gwendolyn led them deeper into the darkened room. The store became an obstacle course with Conner and Nedra struggling to maneuver their way around the trash and debris strewn about the floor.

Gwendolyn finally reached the rear of the store where a closed door awaited. She opened it and held it open, allowing the couple to enter another part of the business. Once all were inside, Gwendolyn flipped a light switch.

The illuminated room proved to be a storage room half the size of the retail part of the store. But unlike the store, this storage room was clean and maintained. There were empty shelves along the walls, several tables, chairs, and a refrigerator. Gwendolyn looked at the couple with hopeful eyes. "Well, this is it. What do you think? Is it okay? I hope it's okay."

Nedra's eyes welled with tears. "This is just what we prayed for. Thank you. Thank you so much."

Connor agreed. "God bless you for what you've done for us. Thank you."

Gwendolyn seemed relieved. "Fantastic. It's great for me, too, because I can still generate some kind of income while I figure out what to do with the place and all the stuff left behind."

Gwendolyn watched as Nedra and Connor positioned the dolly beside a table and removed boxes. Gwendolyn was in her seventies but seemed much younger. She wore her hair in pigtails, and it suited her, as did her outfit. She wore the yellow tracksuit made famous by Bruce Lee in the film *Game of Death*, though the footwear differed—she wore yellow mules. Her meticulous makeup and excellent posture suggested she might have been a showgirl back in the day. She seemed in awe of Connor and Nedra.

"It's such a blessing to have found this place," said Nedra, as she placed a box on a table. "We only need a small amount of space for a short time—time enough to assemble the materials needed for our missionary work. A long-term lease would have been out of the question for us."

Gwendolyn was disappointed. "Too bad, too, because you're just the kind of people I'd want for long-term tenants. It's so difficult to find decent, honest, reliable people these days, especially in Las Vegas. But when I first met you two, I was convinced you were perfect. And my instincts are never wrong." Gwendolyn laughed. "The way things are these days, someone else might try and turn this place into a meth lab!"

"Drugs? Oh, my goodness," answered Nedra.

"Las Vegas is wack," Gwendolyn continued. "But sometimes, you get lucky. And I sure got lucky with you two. I've got an idea. Hear me out and see what you think. The previous tenant bailed out on me some time ago. Long story. My attorney is dealing with him. The problem is, I don't have the time or the knowledge to deal with all the stuff that's been left behind. There's a ton of it. I've got my hands full as it is. But there's something about you two, something so special. I know good, honest people when I meet them. So, I was thinking, I'll make you a deal. You young people are so savvy with your eBay and Craigslist and Napster Chat. Once you get settled in and have some time, I want you to have a look around. If you find something of value around here, I'll split any profit with you fifty/fifty. What do you think?"

Nedra was elated. "Oh, that's so very kind of you! Perhaps we'll take you up on your offer. We could certainly use the extra money for our work. That's such a sweet thought. Thank you for offering."

"Oh, yes," Connor agreed. "God bless you for what you've done for us. Thank you."

"Oh, no, thank you. Thank you, both. You'd be helping me out, that's for sure." Gwendolyn handed two keys to Nedra. "Here are the keys."

Nedra removed an envelope from her purse and handed it to Gwendolyn. "Make sure it's all there."

Gwendolyn didn't bother to open it. "Don't be silly. I know it's all there."

Nedra and Connor stood side-by-side, looking like the children—or perhaps even the grandchildren—that Gwendolyn would have dreamed of having. Gwendolyn first offered them her hand but changed her mind. Instead, she embraced them both, and they reciprocated. Connor even kissed Gwendolyn's cheek, then stepped back, embarrassed by his show of emotion.

"I just wish there were more young people like you in this world," Gwendolyn commented. "It would be a far better place, that's for sure. Anyway, if you need anything, you've got all my contact information. I do check my email every day. I'm not as tech savvy as you young people, but I'm getting there. So that's it. We're all set. I've got to meet with another client, then head back up to Pahrump. I'll lock up behind me."

The three said their goodbyes, and Gwendolyn exited the storage room. Nedra and Connor pressed their ears against the door and listened. When they finally heard the sound of Gwendolyn locking the front door, they smiled at each other like naughty children. And naughty they were indeed.

Nedra and Connor stripped out of the confines of their Christian clothing down to their underwear. Both were heavily decorated with colorful and elaborate tattoos. They opened a couple of boxes, removed clothing, and slipped into different outfits altogether. Their true style sense was a colorful mélange of gypsy, pirate, and Hell's Angel.

Leather was the preferred fabric. Connor was rail thin with an androgynous look accentuated by heavy guyliner. He fashioned his short hair into spikes, courtesy of hair spray. Nedra undid the constricting bun holding her hair hostage, unleashing a wild mane that hung down past her shoulders. The visual contrast between their conservative facade and their dark reality was startling. The sudden roar of thunder somehow served to signify that the transformation was now officially complete.

Once appropriately suited and booted, Nedra and Connor set about unpacking the other boxes. They removed an unusual variety of items that had seemingly no connection to one another—items as crazily diverse as propane tanks, drain cleaner, paint thinner, hotplates, electric frying pans, bottles with rubber tubing attached, cat litter, coffee filters, and multiple boxes of cold tablets.

However, the laboratory beakers, assorted glassware and measuring tools provided an indication of this storage room's actual intent. They worked with the focused efficiency of a well-seasoned team, covering the several available tables and wall shelves with the items. They weren't haphazard in their work, as the items were positioned and placed with aesthetic precision. Soon, the entire storage room had been completely transformed into a state-of-the-art meth lab; what law enforcement officials commonly refer to as a superlab. Nedra and Connor were the Jobs and Woz of meth production and distribution. And they were insanely great.

One table remained clear of meth contraband, and it served as a shared desk for the two renegades. With the unpacking complete, and the lab now prepared for business, Nedra and Connor were free to kick back, sitting at opposite ends of the table. Both were engrossed in their respective laptops with Connor watching *The Twilight Zone* on YouTube, as Nedra scrutinized eBay listings. It was unclear from their body language if they were even a couple. They exchanged no intimacies of any kind. Even now, as they sat at the table, they appeared oblivious to each other.

They were a study in contrasts. Connor removed a skull-shaped mask from a box on the table and attached a pipe to the mouth. He packed the bowl with weed, then placed the mask over his face and lit the bowl. After taking a huge hit, the eyes of the mask turned bright red and sparkled, He exhaled, engulfing himself in smoke.

Nedra's drug use was more subdued and measured. She took a small toke from a one-hitter while making notations about a particular eBay item. Though both did drugs, they confined themselves to marijuana. Ironically, they were manufacturers and distributors of meth, but not tweakers themselves.

A bottle of Jack Daniels, two shot glasses, and a gigantic, frosted cupcake sat in the middle of the table. Connor poured some Jack into a glass and slid it across the table to Nedra, who took a small sip. Nedra sliced a small wedge of cupcake and placed it on a napkin for herself, then pushed the rest of the treat over to Connor, who tore into it immediately. The bottle of Jack sat in his lap. With eyes glued to their individual screens, they barely looked at each other throughout this entire exchange.

Nedra took another sip, then directed her attention away from eBay and over to Connor. "First thing in the morning, we're going next door and doing a little prospecting. Granny Pigtails didn't do that. I've got a feeling there's money over there, whatever that joint was." Nedra watched Connor finish the last of the cupcake. "Can I get you something to eat?"

Connor licked his fingers. "I eat when I'm nervous. You know that. I hate Vegas. I'm ready to get out of here."

"Relax. In a month, we'll be out of here. We're going to get a lot done while we're here. And we'll be set up to make some serious bank. We lucked out with this joint."

Connor remained focused on *The Twilight Zone*; an episode called *The After Hours*. Nedra stood, stretched like a dancer, and looked around the room with pride. It was a laboratory worthy of a major drug cartel. Nedra snapped a few pictures with her cellphone, taking care to get the best angles. She thought of Gwendolyn's infallible instincts and smiled. She pocketed her phone, grabbed her shot glass, and explored their new surroundings. Aside from the door leading to the closed business, three other doors beckoned. One door revealed a broom closet, another door, the bathroom. Nedra opened the third door and flipped the switch on the wall. "Now this is interesting."

Nedra entered a photographer's studio. Though she'd turned on the lights, most of the bulbs in the ceiling were missing. As a result, only scattered streams of light pierced the darkness. The studio was lit, but only barely so, and then only in spots. But there was something else. The studio reeked.

"Oh, my God, what is that smell?"

Except for the missing lights in the ceiling, the studio appeared to be well maintained. There were no cobwebs, and the floor was clear of debris. A large, white backdrop hung from the ceiling, surrounded by lights on tripods, hardly an unusual sight in a photo studio. More unusual were the three mannequins. A bald mannequin head attached to a long flexible rod extended up from the floor near the backdrop. A tall, male mannequin dressed in a tuxedo stood opposite the head. Both mannequins were illuminated by light streaming down from the ceiling. A third female mannequin with legs crossed sat in a nearby chair, obscured by shadows.

Across the room sat a long table littered with boxes of varying sizes. They were far more interesting to Nedra. She walked over, rested her shot glass, and set about opening some of the boxes. She was pleased to discover cameras, lenses, and other photographic equipment. She removed her cellphone from her pocket and checked the value of a couple of items. Her larcenous smile broadened.

"I believe we're onto something here."

Connor hovered in the doorway, peering inside. Nedra remained at the table, her eyes fixed upon the treasures spread out before her. "Come check this stuff out," she said.

Connor was focused on the mannequins and didn't seem to hear.

"Hey, can you grace me with your presence over here,

please?" Nedra insisted. "Check this stuff out."

Connor walked over to the table to join Nedra, who looked as though she'd been opening Christmas presents. "Do you have any idea how much money is laying here?" she asked. "The first thing I picked up is worth a couple grand by itself. And it looks to be all high-end stuff, too. We just got lucky again. I can't even believe it."

Connor glanced down at the items strewn all over the table. He didn't seem impressed. The smell in the studio was fierce, and it showed from the frown on his face. "This place stinks."

"Yeah, I know. I wonder what that is?"

With phone in hand, Nedra walked away from the table and over to one of the studio lights near the backdrop. After finding the make and model number, she fed the information into eBay and smiled again.

Connor joined her, his eyes remaining fixed on the mannequins. The bald mannequin's face was lifelike, albeit in a distorted way, with bulging eyes and a wide, gaping smile. The smile wasn't pleasant, but fiendish, like the smile of a demonic clown. The tall tuxedoed mannequin stood at well over six feet and was equally unnerving. His face was less lifelike than the bald mannequin, with that old school, blank, detached, Sears-store look. But his bodily proportions were unusual and different from typical mannequins. They were exaggerated with longer than normal arms and legs. It was an odd design for a mannequin, making him look less human and more like an abstraction.

Mother Nature decided she was in the mood for a full-blown storm, and rain pummeled the roof, accented by crashes of thunder.

Connor couldn't take his eyes off of the mannequins. "What are these things for, anyway?"

Nedra glanced over at the mannequins while inspecting another light. "They're probably used to test out different lighting setups. I doubt they're worth much. Not compared to that stuff over there. The average lens over there is worth *way* more than these things. That table is straight up bank." Nedra laughed. "We'll leave these for Grandma. We're not greedy. Let's take a look around."

Nedra walked off, and Connor was quick to follow. As they passed the female mannequin sitting in the shadows, Nedra paid her no attention, but Connor stared at her. Though less visible than the other two, and little more than a seated silhouette, this mannequin was more mysterious and compelling. The relaxed positioning of her body, particularly the way her legs were crossed, somehow made her seem more realistic and lifelike. Connor followed Nedra into a dimly lit hallway, and they both grimaced from the stench.

"I don't know what that is, but it smells like the previous tenant was Jeffrey Dahmer," said Nedra. "There's something wrong with the plumbing in this joint. They probably can't keep it rented; not long term, anyway, that's for sure. Not smelling like this."

She walked down the hallway. There were three doors— two side-by-side, and one at the end of the hallway. Nedra opened the first door and turned on the light, revealing a tiny bathroom covered with cobwebs. It looked like it hadn't been used in years. She opened the second door, and turned on the light, discovering the remains of what used to be a photographer's darkroom. Like the bathroom, it was filled with cobwebs. Nedra entered the room, her curiosity piqued.

The room's only light was coming from a low-watt, single, bare bulb suspended from the ceiling, which flickered as if there were a short in the cord. Nedra approached a worktable strewn with rusted, cobweb-covered photographic lab gear that hadn't been used in ages. She could tell it was all junk and not worth the examination.

Connor lingered in the doorway momentarily before entering, his apprehension evident. As he walked deeper into the room, the door slowly closed behind him, revealing a large hook extending out from the top of the door. Cords of varying length and thickness hung over the hook. Connor spotted an object that seemed out of place—a large barrel covered by a lid sat next to a sink in the corner. He stared but didn't approach.

"Nothing much happening in here," said Nedra. "It's cool. We've got more than enough to keep us occupied." She walked past Connor, opened the door, and entered the hallway again, Connor following.

Nedra led the way to the door at the end of the hallway. She opened it and searched for a light switch. There wasn't one, so she took out her cellphone, aiming the flashlight beam inside. It was a storage closet filled with more mannequins. There were males and females, all dressed in formal wear. The faint light from the cellphone made the mannequins appear to glow in the darkness. Nedra was unfazed by the sight of them. Unlike Nedra, Connor was fazed by the mannequins' appearance, and maintained his distance.

"That's it. Let's go."

Nedra closed the door and headed back up the hallway to the studio, with Connor close behind.

Once back in the studio, Nedra returned to the table of treasures, but Connor stopped dead in his tracks. He looked over at the three mannequins, walking up to the tall one and examining him up and down. Was something different? He approached the bald mannequin extending from the flexible rod. Connor stared at it, then slowly reached out to touch it. The sudden boom of thunder both startled and discouraged him, and he lowered his hand. Connor glanced over at the seated female mannequin sitting in the shadows. Even she seemed different.

"I think I got too high tonight."

Nedra looked up from the camera lens she was examining. "Too high? You?" She laughed.

High or not, Connor was quite right in his suspicions. The female mannequin in the shadows was indeed different. Her legs were crossed differently from before.

"The smell in here is probably making you sick. It's making me sick, too. I'm going to move some of this stuff over to the other room and work in there. You just need some air. We passed a Thai joint coming in here. Go get some fried rice, pad Thai, coconut soup, and some egg rolls. And get some beer, too."

"Sounds good. But what do *you* want?" Connor replied, attempting to mask his unease with a bit of levity.

Nedra rolled her eyes and smiled. "That's more like it. So, hurry up. And don't get lost."

"Don't worry. The last place I want to get lost in is Las Vegas." He hurried out of the studio and seemed glad for the opportunity. "I'll be right back."

"I'm gonna start moving this stuff next door. I'm not dealing with this stench another minute." Nedra glanced around the table, trying to decide which treasures to gather up first. Then she noticed something she hadn't seen before. In the far corner of the studio was a computer workstation. On the desk sat a large, flat screen monitor, a keyboard and mouse, and stacks of portable hard drives. A comfortable chair sat in front of the desk.

Nedra walked over and seated herself. She reached over to examine one of the drives, and her hand bumped the mouse, causing the monitor to spring to life. A single folder sat dead center on the computer screen. Nedra clicked on the folder, opening a slideshow photo program. The first photo filled the entire screen, and Nedra was stunned by the sight.

Onscreen was a close-up photo of a man's face. Was he dead? It was hard to tell. The features were contorted, with Ping-Pong eyeballs and a mouth frozen in an agonized scream. It was a nightmare face. This man was living a nightmare, and some photographer had captured the moment. Was he dead? Was this the face of death, or the face of *madness* before death?

Nedra scrolled through the slideshow and discovered

many more such photos, images of men, women, and even children. All faces of madness. She was riveted by the images. What could these people have seen? Whatever it was, it left a lasting impression of horror on their faces. It left an impression on Nedra, as well. She wasn't so cool anymore. She looked traumatized. She didn't feel so lucky anymore, either. A crash of thunder made her jump. A faint sound—a squeak—came from the left, the direction of the mannequins. Nedra whipped her head around to investigate. A hand reached out of the shadows behind her and snatched her by the hair. She screamed.

* * *

Connor unlocked the door of the retail part of the store and entered, carrying a bag of food, drenched from the rain. It had been dusk when they first arrived. Now it was nighttime, which made the store considerably darker.

Connor locked the door behind him, then removed his cellphone, putting it in flashlight mode. He navigated his way through the store, sidestepping the debris, until he reached the door leading to the storage room/superlab. He entered and was surprised not to see Nedra. In fact, it looked as though she'd never come back from the studio at all. No equipment had been brought over. Connor placed the bag of food on the desk.

"Nedra? I'm back." His voice was loud enough to be heard, but there was no answer. He noticed that the door to the studio was closed. He walked over but, rather than opening the door, he just stood beside it. "Nedra? You in there? I'm back." He waited, hoping for the answer that did not come. The only sound was the raging storm. "Nedra?"

Connor opened the door and peered inside. Nedra wasn't in the studio, and the table of treasures looked untouched from earlier. Connor glanced over at the mannequins. They looked the same as well. Everything was the same, except for Nedra's absence. Where was she?

"Where are you?" Connor remained in the doorway, his words sounding like a plea. Still no answer. He entered and walked deeper into the studio. He looked over at the mannequins, then looked away. He entered the hallway but paused before continuing. "Nedra? Are you here?" There was desperation in his plea now. He didn't want to go any further. The intensity of the storm mirrored his growing dread.

Connor walked over to the first door, the bathroom, and opened it. A mirror sat opposite the door. When Connor turned on the light, he was greeted by the unexpected, instantaneous sight of his own reflection and jumped. He turned off the light, closed the door, and continued on to the door of the darkroom. "Nedra?"

Connor opened the door. He made sure to turn on the flickering bare bulb before taking one step inside the room. The room was empty. But there was a sound coming from the corner where the barrel sat beside the sink. The metallic sink had a leaking faucet. When the intermittent drops of water struck the sink, the sound reverberated throughout the room with the insistent rhythm of a human heart.

As Connor approached the sink, he was oblivious to the

darkroom door closing behind him. He reached the sink and stared at the faucet knobs, as if trying to decide whether or not to put a stop to the persistent dripping. As he pondered, a large spider dropped directly in front of his face, suspended by a strand of web. Conner stepped back. The lid of the barrel was knocked away and a figure sprung up like a Jack in the box, covered with thick, smoking liquid. The figure used to be human, but now it was mostly skeleton, with some bits of tendons and flesh still attached. The face was eaten away to the bone, yet somehow the eyes were intact, and the jaw moved as if trying to speak. Though quite dead, the skeleton was fully animated, flailing its arms as if alive.

Connor screamed, then ran backward, away from the barrel, back toward the door. His back slammed into an inert figure suspended from the hook on the door. The figure sprung to life with a shriek and used both arms and legs to seize Connor in a vise-like grip. It was Nedra, or rather used to be. Now she was little more than near-dead flesh moving reflexively. She clung to Connor and wasn't letting go. Connor wasn't staying. He managed to break free from her entwined limbs and twisted out of her grip, even as she clawed at him. Connor flung the door open, as Nedra thrashed on the hook. He ran out of the darkroom and into the hallway where he stumbled and fell to the floor.

The door at the end of the hallway burst open, and out they emerged—the mannequins. They stepped out of the closet one by one, moving in a stiff, robotic, herky-jerky fashion.

Connor was paralyzed as the mannequins gathered en

masse, advancing toward him as if in no hurry. On the floor, he slid back and away from the approaching horde in wide-eyed horror. He climbed to his feet and sprinted up the hallway, back into the studio.

The bald mannequin was alive. The rod attached to its head was now fully extended some five feet or more, and the head bobbed and weaved back and forth with frenzy. Connor stood frozen. The group of mannequins now entered the studio, moving as one.

"Take him!" screamed the bald mannequin.

The tall mannequin stepped out from the shadows behind Connor, snatched him by the back of the collar, and hoisted him off the ground effortlessly, waving him like a captured animal. Connor's feet dangled as the tall mannequin carried him, one handed, over to the backdrop where a chair had been placed. He hurled Connor into the chair, nearly knocking him backward.

The group of mannequins approached and surrounded Connor. He leaped up, but two mannequins seized him and threw him back. They crouched on either side of him and held him fast to the chair. Other mannequins positioned the studio lights, aiming them at Connor, illuminating him. The mannequins laughed, as the thunder roared.

The seated female mannequin uncrossed her legs and stood. She stepped out of the shadows and into a shaft of light, moving in that same bizarre, herky-jerky manner of the other mannequins. Like the others, she, too, was elegantly dressed. Her hair was pulled back into a tight bun that stretched her face to the extreme. It was a nightmare face.

She had the grin of a gargoyle—toothy and cruel—with black, doll-like eyes sunk deep into her head. A camera dangled from a strap around her neck.

Connor lay sprawled in the chair, held down and surrounded by laughing mannequins. His mouth was open. He wanted to scream. The bald mannequin maneuvered itself through the throng and positioned its face close to Connor. He kissed him repeatedly, and Connor finally managed to scream. The mannequins applauded.

The mannequins stepped aside, allowing the female photographer closer access to Connor. He cowered at the frightful sight of her. She aimed her camera at his face and took several shots from various angles while making minute camera adjustments. Clearly, she wasn't shooting in automatic mode. She was a pro. When she finished, she stepped back and allowed the mannequins to rush in on Connor, and they engulfed him. He screamed for the last time.

* * *

Reuben's voice was confident. "I know clowns are hot these days. They *are* creepy. But I think mannequins run a close second." Reuben was proud of the tale he'd just told. "There's just something so weird about them. They've always creeped me out. I've seen other mannequin stories, but I wanted to do one that was a little different. Like my story doesn't take place in a department store for one thing. We've seen that before. And there's just something cool about living mannequins taking pictures of the people they're freaking out. Faces of madness. Headshots of horror.

I've never seen that before."

Neither had Jill. And like Reuben, she, too, thought mannequins to be the embodiment of creepiness.

It was an inventive easter egg, having one of the future victims watching that famous episode of *The Twilight Zone* that featured living mannequins. Reuben's story had the makings of an old school thrill ride with plenty of jump scares. Jill loved the story and agreed with Reuben's creative decisions. Reuben had worked magic, and Jill had captured that magic with ruthless efficiency. The closed briefcase at her side made for an excellent emergency desk. That desk was now covered with 8 x10 cards filled with detailed notes.

Reuben continued with enthusiasm. "I suppose it's kind of a haunted house story. You've got this dark, spooky joint with doors, hallways, cobwebs, and freaky mannequins running around. The way the story unfolds, you just know something wack is gonna go down, you just don't know how. And when it does go down, it's like nothing you've ever seen before. Oh, yeah—I see it in black and white, too. Black and white would emphasize the creep factor big time. Plus, we need to see more stuff in black and white, anyway." Reuben paused as he awaited validating feedback. "So, there it is. What do you think?"

Jill inspected her notes, as she mentally prepared her duplicitous response. "That's pretty good, Reuben."

Reuben awaited further feedback, but it didn't come. "Pretty good? Just pretty good?" From his tone, it was clear he was both surprised and a bit disappointed by Jill's lackluster response.

Jill went back into character, as her plot thickened. "I liked it, Reuben. Honest. I really did. You've got some wonderful ideas, fascinating characters, and great plot devices. Really. If I seem less than blown away, it's probably due to something you said yourself. It's a haunted house story—more or less. In all honesty, I think that type of story might seem kind of… dated. Especially these days. Your story is very good, but it's very moody, too. I think the modern audience is looking for a different kind of horror. Maybe less moody and more, I don't know… up front."

Reuben was silent, and his disappointment with Jill's feedback could be felt through the partition wall. He was proud of his story, and rightly so. Jill's response was not the one he expected to hear. As the silence continued, Jill looked concerned. She certainly wanted to hear more of Reuben's ideas. But her performance in the back of the limo was part theater and part poker. She had just played her hand. If she'd played it correctly, Reuben would continue with more determination. Jill proved to be lucky.

"Well, I've got another story," Reuben began. "It's a lot different. It's not a ghost story at all. More of a dysfunctional family horror story. It's a little more grounded in reality. It's got some characters we've never seen before, especially the villain, if you can call her that. She's like nothing we've ever seen before. But it's pretty scary; at least I think so."

Jill was relieved. She had read Reuben correctly. He knew he was talented, and he was determined to impress her. Little did he know how well he'd succeeded. She gathered up the note cards for Reuben's mannequin story and secured them with a rubber band. She placed the story in her briefcase, as she prepared a fresh set of cards.

"Go ahead, Reuben. I'm all ears."

Lulu's Back in Town

Rocky was well into his seventies, and like many Vegas old schoolers, he still radiated youth. His snow-white hair hung past his shoulders and was pulled back into a ponytail. He wore an AC/DC T-shirt. He had the impish smile of a naughty schoolboy, and it rarely left his face. Rocky had driven a cab in Las Vegas for over forty years. He took great pride in his driving skills and his people skills, considering himself an expert at both. He could read a passenger as well as he could read traffic.

It was rush hour, and the traffic on Patrick Avenue was typical Friday bumper-to-bumper madness, especially near McCarran Airport. Today, the driving was more manic than usual. There was urgency in the air and most of the drivers seemed stressed. As Rocky glanced in the rearview mirror, he could read the stress in the back seat as well.

Tatum looked out the passenger window, indifferent to the gridlock. He was in no hurry to reach his destination, and the longer it took to get there, the better. The sight of familiar landmarks only reinforced the painful reality. Tatum was back in Las Vegas again, and he was going *home*—the last place in the world he wanted to be. His mind was a whirlpool of bleak thoughts, all dragging him round and round, down and down. At least the driver wasn't chatty and bothering him with conversation. Conversation was the last thing Tatum wanted now.

"You don't mind a little conversation, do you?" Rocky was intrigued by his passenger. He was in a chatty mood, too.

Tatum braced himself. "Not at all."

"What's your name?"

"Tatum Witherspoon."

"Well, I'm Rocky Taylor. Very nice to meet you, Tatum. Very nice, indeed. In my business, I meet all kinds of people. And you look like a really fascinating guy. I'm like Sherlock Holmes when it comes to people. I'm a master of deduction. It's a gift. Sometimes, I think I missed my true calling."

"Really? That sounds very interesting." Tatum had zero interest in Rocky's gift or true calling. He made sure that he sounded as uninterested as possible. Unfortunately for Tatum, Rocky was too cheerful to pick up the vibe.

"Other than giving me your address, you haven't said a single word since I picked you up. But I've got a gift. I bet I can tell you a lot about yourself. Mind if I give it a shot?"

"Go ahead. Knock yourself out."

Rocky checked Tatum in the rearview. "Well, let's see. You're from Vegas, but you've been gone a long time. Probably many years. You don't care much for the city. You actually *hate* it, so you're not too keen on being back. You're here against your will... more or less, like for some kind of family business you can't get out of. Something like that. But as soon as you're done with your business, you'll be out of here on the first thing smoking. Las Vegas is the last place you want to be."

Tatum didn't respond, but he was listening.

"You're some kind of artist. Not quite sure what. You're probably a jack and can do a lot of things. You look musical. You're not carrying an instrument, but that doesn't mean you don't play something. You might play piano. You're named Tatum. With your age and ethnicity, your parents were probably jazz fans and named you after Art Tatum, the jazz pianist. But with that body and that perfect posture, you're probably a dancer."

Tatum directed his gaze to Rocky and away from the traffic.

"You've got an unusual style. It's American, but it's European, too. I'd call it *AfroEuro*. There's some Hendrix, some Bowie, some Josephine Baker—along with your own unique flavor, of course. You're an original. The way you dress reflects your mentality. You don't run with the herd. Your clothes are absolutely fabulous, by the way. And you probably designed them yourself. Nobody is looking like that over here. And definitely none of the brothers."

Tatum laughed.

"You've traveled the world, but you make your home in either the U.K. or France. Probably France. Yeah, you'd blossom in a place like France. You'd be right at home. It's the Euro to your Afro. They'd appreciate your flavor over there. You're not famous, but in France, you'd think you were. People probably ask you for autographs because you just look like a celebrity."

Tatum looked back toward the traffic, but his mind was overseas.

"But now, you're in Las Vegas—the last place you want to be. I can understand why you're so sad back there. You may have been born here, but you're a long way from home."

Tatum half-expected Rocky to tell him his preferred sexual position or if he were a top or a bottom… and Rocky would have been right. Rocky proved to be prescient, and his assessment was bull's eye accurate. Tatum was convinced.

"So, what brought you back to Las Vegas?"

"Family business, just like you said. It's the only thing that could bring me back. My mother is sick—it's called advanced vascular dementia, kind of like Alzheimer's. The end result is the same. Her brain is fried and nobody's home. She's been living in a nursing facility for years, but we had to move her out because the place is going out of business. We've moved her back to the family home temporarily."

"We?"

"Me and my sister, Hazel. She lives in Boulder City. She's a realtor, and she's on the road a lot. I came back to help take care of my mom until we can find a new place to put her in."

"How long will you have to be here?"

"I don't know. As long as it takes, I guess. I just hope I've got some sanity left when it comes time to leave."

Rocky turned onto Tatum's street and slowed as he scanned the addresses. It was a well maintained, affluent neighborhood with lots of trees and greenery. Tatum pointed toward a house, and Rocky parked in front, leaving the motor running. The house was an impressive brick, two-story structure that sat several yards back from the sidewalk. The two trees in the front yard were dead, as were the many shrubs and bushes that surrounded the house. Even the grass was dead. The house looked as though no one had lived there for some time.

Tatum reached for his wallet. "I know you can read people. What about houses? This is where I grew up. What do you think?"

Rocky looked at the house. Though it was similar architecturally with the other houses in the neighborhood, it seemed so out of place. The other houses showed obvious signs of life. This house was clearly dead, and it stood out like a mausoleum. A tumbleweed rolled by, accentuating the sense of desolation.

Tatum handed Rocky two twenty-dollar bills. "Keep it."

Rocky turned to face Tatum as he took the money. He looked concerned. "Thank you. And I don't like it. The sooner you're out of here, the better." It sounded like a warning.

Tatum laughed, but he found Rocky's distinct change in personality a bit unsettling. They both climbed out of the cab. Rocky opened the trunk and removed the suitcase.

"Thanks for the tip. I really appreciate it. Take care of yourself."

"My pleasure. Best of luck to you."

The two men shook hands. Rocky climbed back inside the cab and drove off. Tatum stood staring at the house that towered before him. It was now official. He was home. The last place in the world he wanted to be.

Tatum picked up his suitcase and made his way up the stone walkway to the front door. He entered the house, set down his suitcase, and closed the door behind him. The house was illuminated by the late day sun shining through curtained windows. The foyer was dominated by a wide staircase with red carpet that ascended before him. At the bottom of the staircase was a tall floor lamp missing a lampshade. The lamp was turned off.

Tatum walked into the living room. All of the furniture was covered by canvas tarpaulins. Tatum's eyes were drawn to the grand piano which, though covered, still commanded the room. He continued on to the kitchen. The sink, stove, refrigerator, and countertop looked to have been recently cleaned. In the middle of the room was a canvas-covered dining table and chairs.

Tatum exited the kitchen and walked down a hallway. A door at the end was slightly ajar. He pushed it open. There were no windows, so the room was near dark. It had once been a den. Now, there was a bed and nightstand in the corner. Nearby was a door to the bathroom. A television sat on a table against the wall. The television volume was low, but loud enough to be heard, and its glow provided the only light in the room. Tatum's mother, Dorinda, sat in a comfortable chair in the middle of the room, facing the television.

Dressed in a white linen nightgown and slippers, she was old, black, and frail. Her sunken eyes were open wide, but they lacked cognition. Though she faced the television, she wasn't really looking at it, but rather through it. She could just as well have been staring at the wall. She was bald except for a few thin strands of white hair that hung on the sides and down the back. A smile was fixed upon her face, as if she were replaying some old joke in her head. Oddly, she wore an abundance of makeup: thick black eyeliner, eyelashes, red cheek rouge, and red lipstick. It was crude, garish, and looked as if she had applied it herself.

Tatum entered the room and walked closer to his mother, or rather to this new person who only vaguely resembled the woman he had once known. He hadn't seen his mother in several years, before the series of strokes transformed her into the human husk sitting before him now. Back then, she was heavier, with a full head of hair, a perfectly made-up face, and life in her eyes. Tatum stared at the person in the chair and struggled to convince himself that it was indeed his mother. She almost looked like a man trying to look like a woman without success. The makeup was grotesque, making her appear more fiendish than female.

The bathroom door opened, and a shriek startled both Tatum and Dorinda. A Mexican woman dressed in pink stood in the doorway, terrified by the unexpected sight of Tatum. Dorinda burst into laughter and clapped her hands with glee. "Okey doke, okey doke!" She followed the exclamations by mimicking parrot whistles.

"It's okay," Tatum said, addressing the startled woman. "I'm Tatum. My plane was delayed. I just got here."

Tatum's tone was reassuring, but the woman, a home health aide, still appeared distressed. Her name was Lupe.

"Where's my sister?" Tatum added. "Isn't she here, yet?"

"She not here. I go now. I go." Lupe's tone was not reassuring, and Tatum's introduction did little to quell her fear. Lupe snatched her purse from the nightstand, then rushed past Tatum and out of the room, heading up the hallway as if making an escape. Confused, Tatum followed after her.

"Hey. Wait a minute. Where are you going?"

Lupe hurried out of the kitchen and into the living room as she pulled car keys from her purse. She was at the front door when Tatum reached her.

"Wait. Why are you leaving? You're supposed to be here with me and my mother. You can't leave."

"You here now. I go!" Something other than Tatum's unexpected appearance had caused her alarm.

"You can't leave. I can't take care of her by myself."

"I go now! She crazy!" Lupe was frantic and wouldn't be dissuaded. She opened the door and dashed out of the house.

Tatum stood in the doorway, bewildered. Then he got pissed. He slammed the door and stormed back to the kitchen while pressing digits into his cellphone. The cheerful recorded response increased his agitation.

"Hello. You've reached Hazel Witherspoon. I'm out and about, but give me a shout after the beep. Bye!"

Tatum ended the call without leaving a message. Exasperated, he snatched the canvas coverings away from the kitchen table and chairs, rolled them into a ball, and hurled it into a corner with an expletive. He wanted to break something. Finally, he sat down, placed the phone on the table, and took a deep breath to calm himself. The phone rang and he answered, putting the phone on speaker.

"Where are you?" Tatum was determined to stay calm.

"Something came up. I'm running late." The volume was turned all the way up, and Hazel's voice could be heard loud and clear. "How was your flight? Is everything—?"

"No, everything is *not* okay. The nursing aide or assistant or whatever just walked out. Ran out. No reason, no explanation, no nothing."

"What?"

"That's right, so you'd better call somebody and find out what's going on. Call them right now—this minute."

Tatum ended the call. Things weren't off to a good start. He hadn't been home for five minutes, and he already had major problems. What could have made that woman run out like that? The phone rang, and he answered, keeping it on speaker mode.

"So, what's going on?" he asked.

"I just called," Hazel said nonchalantly, "but it's after six. No one answered, so the office must be closed for the day."

"What?" Tatum's anger was ignited again. "Well, you'd better find a different number and call that. Somebody is supposed to be here, but nobody is here!"

"Can you relax long enough to help me understand what's going on?"

"I'm about as relaxed as I'm going to get. First of all, you were supposed to be here. Second, you told me there would be an aide or whatever helping out. Where are you, anyway?"

"I just told you, something came up. And somebody *is* supposed to be there. I haven't screwed up anything. I arranged this thing like a military campaign. I had her transferred from the nursing joint this morning. The agency I hired brought her back home and got her settled in. I had hoped to be there by the time you got to town. Something came up. But like I said, I took care of it. Somebody is supposed to be there now."

"Well, nobody *is* here now. Do you understand what I'm saying? There was some goofy chick here when I got here, but she split. She ran out the door like the house was on fire. What am I supposed—?"

"Listen, Tatum, I'll try and find out what's going on, but until I do, you're going to have to maintain."

"Maintain? How the hell am I supposed to do that? I don't know how to deal with this situation. I'm no caregiver or caretaker or whatever. What am I supposed to do when she's got to go to the bathroom?"

"Then take her. She can walk a little bit."

Tatum stood up from the table. His frustration was getting the best of him, and he needed to move.

"Look, Hazel, I can't deal with this. Do you understand me? You can't just throw me into this shit and expect me to start swimming."

"I don't know what else to tell you for now. You're just going—"

"You tell me to maintain one more time and—"

"I'll try and find some kind of emergency number. There's got to be some—"

"You do that. And then you get here as soon as you can. I can't deal with this by myself, and I'm not about to try."

Tatum ended the call with an expletive. He considered kicking one of the chairs but maintained himself. He glanced toward the hallway. He wasn't ready to deal with Dorinda just yet. He needed to get his head together first. He walked out of the kitchen and into the living room, and again his gaze fell upon the covered grand piano. He walked over to it. Maybe it would help to chill him out a bit while he waited for Hazel. He pulled off the covering, tossed it aside, and seated himself.

As he warmed up with a few scales, he frowned with familiar displeasure. He hated this piano. Aside from now being out of tune, the piano was a bitch to play and always had been. The keys were as stiff and unmanageable as ever. The piano was a beautiful piece of furniture, but virtually impossible to play … at least for him.

Of course, Dorinda never had a problem playing this piano. She loved it and played it obsessively. It was perfect for her. For one thing, she had unusually large hands. Tatum once saw her effortlessly pick up a basketball with one hand. In addition to having hands like an NBA player, she was incredibly strong.

Dorinda had been a formidable pianist. Tatum wasn't nearly as skilled as his mother, but he was proficient, favoring show tunes. He struggled to play them on this instrument, a piano he used to call the hand breaker. He stopped playing and massaged his fingers.

Tatum's cellphone remained in the kitchen. When it

rang, he leapt up from the piano and ran to answer it. Seating himself, he left the phone on the table and talked on speaker.

"Okay, so what's going on?" Tatum tried to sound hopeful.

"I called another number, and left a detailed message, but no one has called back yet. There's something else, though. I won't be able to get there today."

Tatum stood. "What? Are you kidding me? You'd better not be serious."

"Look, Tatum, I'm not even in Vegas. At the moment, I'm still in Cali. I thought I'd be back by the time you got in, but something came—"

"This is bullshit, Hazel! All of it. Everybody that's supposed to be here is gone—except me."

"I'm sorry, but it is what it is. There's nothing else I can do about anything right now."

"So just when do you plan on getting here?"

"I can't even say for sure right now. It's a business thing. I'm dealing with a client. This is an important deal and I'm—"

Tatum had heard enough. He ended the call, fighting the urge to slam the phone against the wall. Instead, he kicked one of the chairs with an expletive, sending it rolling across the kitchen. He then heard the sound of laughter, bird whistles, and clapping coming from Dorinda's room down the hall. The room was in earshot of the kitchen, and Dorinda was clearly amused by all she'd heard. Her reaction enraged Tatum all the more, and he debated whether or not to kick another chair.

Tatum needed a drink. He searched the kitchen, opening cabinets, but found only glasses, dishes, and other kitchenware. He opened the refrigerator to find a six-pack of Ensure and a jar of applesauce. He was ready to rip the refrigerator door from its hinges, but instead merely closed it… delicately. Hazel was right. He had better maintain. If he didn't find some way to stay Zen, he'd end up destroying the whole house. That's what the rage was all about, anyway, and he knew it. He was home again—the last place he wanted to be. He was ready to tear the house down completely.

Tatum snatched the cellphone off the table and put it in his pocket. He walked out of the kitchen, into the living room, and out into the foyer. Maybe exploring the rest of the house would help to chill him out.

As he ascended the stairs, he looked at the many familiar pictures that lined the wall. He hadn't seen them in years. They were all pictures of Dorinda Witherspoon the way she used to be. Back in the day, she had been one of the most popular cocktail pianists in Las Vegas and was a favorite with celebrities. The first picture was a poster of her dressed in red, her favorite picture. The wall stood as a sad shrine to Dorinda and her career. The vibrant woman in the pictures looked nothing like the frightening figure in the den.

There were four closed doors on the second floor. Tatum opened the first door, revealing a bathroom. The second door led to a bedroom that had been converted to a storage room filled with boxes. Mattresses and bedframes leaned against the wall. The third door revealed another converted bedroom, this one used for storing clothes. There were several long racks placed throughout the room, all lined with clothes in vinyl protective covering.

Tatum proceeded to the fourth and final door and opened it. It had been Dorinda's bedroom and was still intact with a bed, nightstand, and dresser. The bed appeared to have been recently made with fresh linen and a bedspread. Apparently, this room was to serve as his room for the duration of his stay.

Tatum headed back downstairs and saw there was less light than when he'd first arrived. The sun was setting. A light switch beside the front door illuminated the foyer, but Tatum discovered the light didn't work. He went into the living room and flipped the light switch. Again, the light didn't work. An enormous picture window beside the piano provided the waning sunlight to the room.

Tatum returned to the kitchen and flipped the light switch. The room lit up to his surprise and relief. He looked toward the hallway. No need to venture back down there just yet. He already knew the electricity was working in Dorinda's temporary room. Clearly, something wack was going on with the house electricity since it wasn't working in every room. Just one more problem to add to the list.

Tatum sat at the table, activated his phone, and searched online for an Indian restaurant. He found one nearby that delivered and placed an order, making sure to include some Indian beer. He needed to alter his consciousness immediately, and it would be a while before the liquor arrived. He needed a quick fix and went back to the foyer to retrieve his suitcase. Before he headed upstairs, he turned on the floor lamp at the foot of the stairs. Fortunately, it worked, though the bulb was a bit dim. The lamp was a five-foot-tall brass pole with no shade at the top and a heavy base. It was an ugly eyesore that didn't belong in that spot. But the odd placement made sense. The lamp was meant to serve as the sole source of light for the entire downstairs entrance area. Tatum left the lamp on.

Tatum headed upstairs to Dorinda's bedroom, which was his new room. He entered and placed his suitcase on the dresser. He opened it and dug deep through the clothes until he found his quick fix. He removed a fake canister of deodorant, unscrewed the cap, and removed a small stash box. It was the first time Tatum had smiled since returning home. A table lamp on the nightstand was beside the bed, and he was elated to find the lamp working.

Stash box in hand, he headed back downstairs to the kitchen and seated himself at the table. He glanced toward the hallway, trying to decide which should come first—Dorinda or the dope. It was a tough call. He needed to get wasted. He deserved it, and the sooner the better. But he was going to have to deal with Dorinda eventually. He might as well deal with her now. There was no avoiding it. He left the stash box on the table and headed down the hallway to the den.

Tatum paused in the doorway and stared at the remains of his mother. Dorinda looked as she had earlier, sitting comfortably confused in front of the television, bathed in its glow. The glow only made her look more eerie with that ghastly made-up face. The sight of her chilled him. The prospect of dealing with her by himself for any length of time even more so.

Tatum entered and sat on a foot stool beside Dorinda's chair, positioning himself facing her with his back to the television. He could barely look at her. She was hideous. Though Tatum was seated in front of her, Dorinda looked right through him as if he were transparent.

"Hey, Mama, it's me, Tatum. I'm home." He made a valiant attempt at sounding pleasant. "You okay? Is everything all right?"

At first, Dorinda had no response. Then a change came over her. Her dark, sunken eyes gradually focused on Tatum. Now, she looked *at* him rather than *through* him, and she seemed to recognize him as well. She nodded, with genuine cognition. Tatum was surprised, though no less creeped out.

"Okey doke, okey doke." Bird whistles followed.

Dorinda stared intently at Tatum. Her eyes were piercing, particularly now that they were focused. She recognized him, all right, but her cognition only increased the creep factor. Tatum then realized that he actually preferred her the other way—vacant and unfocused. That way, she was somewhat *gone*. But now, she was *here*, rather than *there*, and clearly in the moment. Her smile broadened, and her eyes sparkled.

"I'm back. I came back just to see about you. I'll be here for a while, too." Tatum was nauseated by the words but maintained an insincere smile as he spoke them. "Do you know where you are now?"

"Home," she replied. "I'm not leaving. Not this time. Not this time."

Tatum was again surprised. Dorinda was somewhat aware and even articulate. He didn't expect her to be so communicative. He was relieved to know he wouldn't be dealing with a complete vegetable.

"Where's Monk? Where's Monk?" She asked.

Tatum wasn't quite sure how to respond. Monk was her pet parrot from back in the day, like thirty years back in the day. "Uh, he's around someplace. He's okay." It was the only response he could think of on the spot. Luckily, it seemed to suffice.

"Okey doke. Okey doke." Bird whistles followed.

"Can I get you something?"

"Not this time."

Tatum tried to relax. Maybe he just needed to get used to her. It was a challenge with that monstrous makeup, but that strange look in her eyes was just as bad. He felt as if he were under a microscope, being dissected.

Tatum continued. "I played your piano today. We need to get that thing tuned. It sounds terrible."

"I play piano."

"That's right, you play piano."

"And you suck dicks." Dorinda said, laughing at her joke.

Tatum was hardly expecting such a response. "What did you say?"

"You suck dicks. You're a fag like your daddy. Just like your daddy." Bird whistles followed.

Tatum stood and stepped back, allowing the glow of the television full access to Dorinda once again. He stared down at her, astonished by her brazen words. She stared back at him, seemingly well aware of what she'd said. The shock on

Tatum's face tickled her. She seemed to enjoy both his surprise and unease. Dorinda was having fun.

Tatum was too stunned to answer. He didn't want to answer. He just wanted to get out of that room and away from her. He walked over to the doorway, then turned back toward Dorinda. She was looking straight ahead again, sitting in comfortable confusion, staring blankly at the television screen. She was *gone*.

Tatum returned to the kitchen and sat at the table. He stared at the stash box. Now, he wasn't sure he even wanted to get high. He'd just had his mind blown. Could there have been a mistake with her initial diagnosis after the strokes? Was she as far gone as originally thought to be? Doctors misdiagnose all the time. It happens. Dorinda was more than responsive. She was communicative, mindful, and opinionated—in the extreme. Traces of the domineering, smart assed, big mouth bitch he remembered from his youth still remained. More than traces. And she was certainly no vegetable. If anything, she was in a heightened state of awareness, regardless of her so-called advanced vascular dementia. It made being in her presence even more chilling.

The sound of the doorbell redirected Tatum's thoughts. He stood and walked out of the brightness of the kitchen into the semi-darkness of the living room. Moonlight shone through the picture window, illuminating the grand piano. Tatum stepped into the dim light of the foyer and opened the front door. A young deliveryman stood holding a large paper bag. The sight of Tatum brought a curious smile to his face.

"Witherspoon?" The deliveryman eyed Tatum up and down admiringly.

"That's me." Tatum handed the man a fifty-dollar bill and took the food. "Keep it."

"Thanks a lot. I really like your style by the way. You're not from here, are you?"

"Born and raised, unfortunately. Just moved back. I'll be around for a while."

"Well, that's really good to know. We're open till 3 A.M., just so you know. If you order again, and I see your name, I'll deliver it myself."

"I'll keep that in mind. Thanks."

"No—thank you."

The deliveryman headed back to his car, and Tatum closed the door. As he walked back to the kitchen, he looked inside the bag, and his displeasure was immediate.

"Great, they forgot the beer."

Tatum set the bag down on the table, reached for his cellphone, and called the restaurant. The apologetic manager was sincerely sorry for the mistake and promised to send the beer over right away. He also offered to send over something extra just to make things right. Tatum wasn't particularly angry about the goof up. The prospect of another delivery was actually exciting. In the meantime, he'd give Dorinda some dinner. He washed his hands, then searched the cabinets for a plate and silverware. He removed the various containers of food from the bag, prepared Dorinda's plate, then headed down the hallway to the den.

It looked as if Dorinda hadn't moved at all. Tatum sat on

the stool beside her and rested the plate in her lap. The aroma of the food seemed to spark her cognition. Dorinda looked down at the plate, sniffed the contents, and smiled. She picked up the fork and ate. Her eyes remained on the television screen.

"I like curry."

"I know you do. That's why I got it."

"You like dicks, just like your daddy."

Tatum shifted the conversation to a different subject. He was curious about the extent of her cognitive abilities. "Where's Hazel? Have you seen Hazel lately?"

"Hazel? She's not here. She's in Cali. She's with a client. You're mad. You kick chairs and say 'fuck'." Dorinda laughed. "You better maintain. You better maintain."

Tatum was too dumbfounded to answer.

Dorinda loved the curry and the conversation. "Hazel likes money. Hazel's full of shit."

Tatum agreed and fought the urge to laugh. Dorinda's capacities were certainly limited, but her level of cognition was amazing. Clearly, some doctor had made a mistake.

"I like curry. You like—"

"Do you want some more rice? There's plenty more in the kitchen."

"Once I came home early. He got busted."

Tatum vibed where this conversation was going and didn't want to go there. Unfortunately, Dorinda wasn't just aware, she was in a chatty mood.

"He was on the bottom. White boy on the top." Dorinda laughed at the memory.

"Is that enough gravy? You want some more, Naan?"

"Your daddy liked white boys. I bet you like white boys, too. Just like your daddy. Do you like—"

"I'd like you to finish your curry before it gets cold."

"You'd like me to shut up. Okey doke, okey doke." Bird whistles followed.

Tatum stood. He'd had enough conversation for now. More than enough. He was ready to get out of there and ready to get wasted.

Dorinda handed Tatum her plate. "I gotta go."

"Go where?" Tatum was afraid of the answer.

"You know, the bathroom. I gotta go. I gotta go now."

Tatum set the plate on the stool and helped Dorinda to stand. He put his arm around her waist and guided her toward the bathroom. She was a bit unsteady, but with Tatum's assistance, she was able to walk to the bathroom successfully. Dorinda hoisted up her nightgown and squatted on the toilet. The sound of a long, loud, mournful fart filled the bathroom, enhanced by the natural acoustics.

"E flat," said Dorinda. "I like that key."

As a disgusted Tatum turned to leave, he noticed the bathroom sink was littered with Dorinda's makeup items. "I'll leave you alone so you can—"

The fart was followed by a fecal faucet turned full blast. Soon, the bathroom reeked, and Tatum frowned with disgust.

"All done. You gotta help."

"Help what?" Tatum was afraid of the answer.

"Wipe."

Tatum was nauseated by the prospect. He desperately scanned the bathroom for a box of rubber gloves. Surely there were rubber gloves. He saw only the makeup and liquid soap on the sink. He checked the cabinets above and below the sink, and both were empty. There were no rubber gloves.

"Could you flush that, please?"

Dorinda laughed. "It's bad." She flushed the toilet. "All gone." She pulled a significant amount of toilet paper from the roll and handed it to Tatum as he watched in horror.

Dorinda rose from the toilet on her own and bent forward, allowing easier access to her ass. Tatum pulled up his sleeves past the elbows. He positioned one hand on her ass, using his fingers to separate both cheeks simultaneously. This gave his other hand holding the toilet paper total freedom to work. It was a skillful move for a first-timer.

"You've spread cheeks before. Just like your daddy."

Tatum wiped Dorinda clean, but she wasn't satisfied. She unrolled more toilet paper and handed it to him. Tatum repeated his skillful moves and flushed. He immediately went over to the sink, turned on the hot water, and let it run as he coated his hands with a third of the contents of the liquid soap bottle. He winced in pain when he placed his hands under the scalding stream of water. He dried his hands on a towel hanging from the wall. As he looked in the mirror, he saw Dorinda standing beside him smiling.

"Okey doke, okey doke."

Tatum led Dorinda out of the bathroom and back over to her chair. As she seated herself, he smelled his fingers for any aromatic remnants. Looking down at her, he had an idea. He went back into the bathroom, removed the towel on the wall, and moistened it with warm water. He returned to Dorinda to deliver the news.

"You'll be going to bed before long. I'm going to clean all that gunk off your face while I'm here."

Tatum bent over to wipe away Dorinda's makeup, but she reached out with one hand, grabbed him firmly by the balls, and twisted. Tatum dropped the towel and screamed. Even using both of his hands, he couldn't free himself from her strong, vise-like grip.

Dorinda was amused by Tatum's frantic attempts to break free from her. "You dance like a fag. Just like your daddy."

Tatum finally broke free. He ran to the doorway, then turned back to look at her. Dorinda was turned in his direction, and her eyes were blazing. She wasn't smiling. "Not this time." Dorinda turned back to the television.

Tatum returned to the kitchen and called Hazel.

"Hello. You've reached Hazel Witherspoon. I'm out and about but give me a shout after the beep. Bye!"

Tatum kicked a chair and sent it rolling with an expletive. He could hear Dorinda down the hall, laughing and clapping.

"You better maintain. You better maintain." Bird whistles followed.

Tatum thought of the Mexican woman who'd fled the house in fear earlier. The doorbell jolted him. He walked out of the kitchen, through the darkened living room, and out to the foyer. He opened the door and found the smiling deliveryman standing before him once more. He was holding another bag.

"Man, I am so sorry about this. I don't know how that happened. But here's the rest of your order. Plus, there's some other goodies in there, too. I hooked you up myself. I am so sorry." As he handed the bag to Tatum, he noticed the residual distress on his face. He was genuinely concerned. Plus, it provided an opportunity to chat. "You okay? You don't look so okay."

"Yeah, I'm fine," replied Tatum. "It's been a long day. I just got back to town. I'm still readjusting."

"Well, speaking of readjusting, I know you like beer. Would you happen to be 420 friendly?"

"As I matter of fact, I am. I brought some back with me, but it won't last. I'll be needing a hookup."

"I can help with that. By the way, I'm Tyler Savage."

"Tatum. Nice to meet you, Tyler."

The two men shook hands. Tyler was half Tatum's age—perhaps even younger—but he was fascinated by the unusual older man standing before him. He wanted to make an impression.

"Seriously, I can get whatever you need. And for the right price, too. Forget about a dispensary. Not with me around. You like moon rocks?"

"Moon rocks?"

Tyler giggled mischievously. "You never had rocks? Oh, my God. Come out to my office this instant."

Tyler took the bag out of Tatum's hands and placed it on the floor beside the door. He beckoned Tatum to follow him, and the two walked out into the night, down the stone walkway to Tyler's parked car. They climbed inside, and Tyler started the engine. He turned on some music, lit a small pipe and handed it to Tatum. Tatum took a deep hit and settled back in his seat as he exhaled. The music was good, and he loved House. As the effects of the moon rocks took hold, Tatum found himself relaxed for the first time since returning to Vegas.

"I feel like dancing."

"I'd like to see that sometime." Tyler jotted numbers inside a matchbook and handed it to Tatum. "Hold onto this. It's a souvenir. I gotta get back to the restaurant."

"Thanks for the lift."

Tatum climbed out of the car. As he shut the door, Tyler handed him a small piece of tin foil through the open window.

"Take that with you. A little parting gift. See ya!"

Tyler drove off with a wave, and the House music could be heard blaring in the distance. Tatum headed back to the other house… his house. But he was in far better spirits now. He entered, closing the door behind him. He picked up the bag beside the door and walked back to the kitchen. The sound of Dorinda's television could be heard down the hall. Tatum placed the bag inside the refrigerator. He needed neither food nor alcohol; at least for the moment. Now, he was totally Zen.

Tatum walked out of the kitchen and into the living room. He removed the canvas coverings from the rest of the furniture and placed them in a corner. The moonlight shining on the piano was a picturesque sight, and he was in such a good mood, he almost felt like playing again. But the thought of dealing with that hand breaker changed his mind. He'd rather be dancing, anyway. He walked out into the foyer and ascended the staircase while singing the Police song, *Walking on the Moon.*

Tatum entered the bedroom. The floor lamp downstairs provided a bit of light at the doorway. The room was near dark, but the vague outlines of the furniture could be seen. Tatum stripped to his underwear and tossed his clothes on top of his suitcase on the dresser, plopping himself on the bed. He didn't know if it was the rocks or what, but he really did feel different, as if he'd achieved some higher level of consciousness. His life was still a mess, but he would deal with it and overcome it. No more rage and kicked chairs. And he'd roll with Dorinda's annoying commentary, too. From now on, no matter what happened, he'd stay Zen. And most of all, he'd maintain.

Tatum sat upright against the headboard and turned on the table lamp beside the bed. Dorinda was sitting beside him, and Tatum screamed at the sudden sight of her. He reflexively backed away from her, falling off the bed and onto the floor. Dorinda moved closer to the edge of the bed and looked down at him. She laughed at the frightened sight of him crawling away on his hands and knees to get away.

"This is my room," she said.

Tatum crawled out of the room, climbed to his feet, and ran down the stairs.

* * *

Hazel arrived the next day close to 6 P.M. She parked her silver Saab and walked up to the front door, carrying a grocery bag. She was a striking woman, dressed for success, who routinely turned heads wherever she went. She agreed with the public opinion of her looks and never met a mirror she didn't like. She entered the house and headed for the kitchen.

"Hazel Witherspoon, in the house. Come out, come out, wherever you are." She was in a merry mood.

Hazel entered the kitchen and found Tatum hard at work behind an ironing board. Shirts and pants were slung over a nearby chair, waiting their turn to be ironed. When Tatum saw her, he acknowledged her with a nod, then continued his work.

"Glad you could make it." Tatum was not in a merry mood.

"What kind of greeting is that?" Hazel set the bag on the kitchen counter and walked over to give Tatum a perfunctory hug. Perfunctory hugs were a Hazel specialty, and she gave them often.

Tatum didn't reciprocate and barely stopped ironing. "Did you get your business settled okay? Did you make that money?"

Hazel moved away from Tatum and his negative vibe. She could sense an argument approaching, the way an airliner approaches a runway, slowly but surely. She busied herself unpacking the items from the grocery bag, awaiting the inevitable touchdown.

"I brought you some stuff." Hazel opened the refrigerator to place food inside. "Oh, great. You picked up a few things already."

"Good thing I did, too. There was nothing here for me when I got here. There was nobody here for me either."

"Tatum, are we going to start again?"

"You'd better believe it. So have a seat."

Hazel put away the last of the groceries and sat at the table. She removed a cellphone from her Vera Wang jacket and checked her messages. There were a string of them, and she glanced at each and every one. When she finally looked up from her phone, Tatum was glaring at her.

"Are you ready now?"

"Please, Tatum, can't we just chill? I'm here now, okay? And I busted my ass to get back here, too. The traffic in Cali was nuts."

"You were supposed to be here yesterday."

Hazel didn't bother to respond. The confrontation was unavoidable. Just like old times.

"So, what's up with whoever is supposed to be here? Let's start with that."

"I finally got through to the agency. Apparently, there were some problems with the aide yesterday."

"I already *know* that, Hazel. *I* was the one who told *you*. Tell me something I don't know. Did they say why she left? Are they sending somebody else to replace her?

"I guess old girl must have grabbed her arm or something, and it freaked her out."

"Are they sending somebody else to replace her?"

"There's no one else available—at least right now. But they referred me to another—"

"Great. I had a feeling you were going to say that. Well, guess what? Until you find a replacement, you've got the job."

"What are you talking about? I've got to go back home. I've got to—"

"Stay right here and deal with this, with me. That's what you've got to do. Besides, this is your home, too. Boulder City can wait. And that's your mother as much as mine."

Hazel became defensive and copped an attitude of her own. "I know exactly who she is. While you've been living in France, doing whatever it is you're doing these days, I've been over here doing—"

"Nothing. That's what you've been doing. Nothing for her, at least. The nursing home was taking care of her, and her pension covered the bills. So don't make it seem like you've been turning backflips for her. You probably never even went to visit her, did you? How long has it been since you've seen her, anyway?"

"I don't know. I don't keep track. Even if I did go to see her, she wouldn't know who I was anyway, so what difference does it make?

"The point is this—we're in this together. I'm not dealing with this alone. And now that you're here, we might as well start tonight. I'm going out."

"What? Who's going to—"

"You are. I need to get out of here tonight, at least for a minute. I'll be back."

"I wasn't planning on staying here tonight."

"And I wasn't planning on dealing with her alone, either.

Plans change all the time. It's called life. Deal with it. You can go back to Boulder City tomorrow, pack a bag, then get back over here. We're in this together. It might give you an incentive to find your replacement. Teamwork makes the dream work."

"Oh, I'll find a replacement, all right."

"You do that. You'll be all right. It's not like we're dealing with something out of the produce section. I think whoever diagnosed her is the one confused. She's no rocket scientist, but she's no vegetable, either—not by a longshot. She's more on point than a lot of people I know. And by Vegas standards, she's Mensa material. She's about the only person I can get a straight answer out of around here. It might not be the answer I want, but it makes sense."

"What are you talking about? That chick barely made sense back in the day. She sure ain't making any sense now."

"She makes all kinds of sense. I can understand every word she says."

"Every word she says? She doesn't say anything."

"What do you know about it? You don't even know when you last saw her. Mama is responsive. She communicates. She can talk all right. Once she gets going, she acts like she doesn't want to shut up."

Hazel laughed. "Are you trippin'? That chick hasn't talked in years. Unless you're calling okey doke a word. Technically, that's two words, and in her condition, she's barely saying that. If she were as verbose as you claim she is, I think I would have heard about it from the nursing home before now."

Tatum placed the iron in an upright position and turned it off. He was angry. "I've got one nerve left, Hazel. Don't get on it, okay? I've been here with her. I know what I'm talking about. She's absolutely aware of what's going on around her. She may be in and out, but she ain't totally gone, that's for damn sure. And she can talk, too. Come on, I'll prove it to you right now. Come on."

Tatum headed down the hallway to the den. Hazel followed, albeit reluctantly. They entered the room and found Dorinda seated in her chair, comfortably confused, facing the television. She was wearing the same nightgown. Her face was still made up, but it looked as though she'd touched it up a bit.

Hazel was unprepared for the sight of her. "Oh, my God. She looks like the Crypt Keeper. She's hideous."

"Haven't seen her in a while, huh? Maybe you need to get reacquainted."

"She always liked her makeup. Some things never change. But damn—look at her. We've got to get her a wig or a hat or something. If I've got to be here, I'm not looking at that. I'm serious."

Tatum pointed at the footstool beside Dorinda's chair. "Go ahead, sit down."

Hazel sat and moved the stool closer to Dorinda. She looked at her mother with detachment, saying nothing, not even 'hello.' Dorinda looked straight ahead. Tatum knelt beside her chair. He glanced over at Hazel, and he was already smiling triumphantly.

"Listen to this. You'll see." Tatum directed his gaze to

Dorinda. "Hey, Mama, is everything all right?"

"Okey doke, okey doke." Bird whistles followed.

"Go ahead. You talk to her. Say something."

Hazel indulged him and leaned closer to her mother. She addressed Dorinda by her childhood nickname, the name favored by her closest of friends. "Hey, Lulu, it's me, Hazel. Hello, hello, is anybody in there? Hello? Knock knock. Who's there? Anybody home? Come out and play. Peek-A-Boo." Hazel's tone was cold and patronizing.

Tatum was irritated. "Just be normal about it." Tatum rested his hand on Dorinda's knee as he addressed her. "Go ahead, Mama, say something. You okay? Is everything all right?"

Dorinda said nothing more and remained oblivious. Tatum looked concerned. Dorinda could certainly speak. Maybe she just needed to be triggered to reach a more responsive state. The right subject matter might really get her going.

"You like curry… I like dicks."

Hazel looked at Tatum in disbelief. Dorinda looked straight ahead and remained silent. Tatum tried again with more determination.

"I suck dicks. I'm a fag, just like daddy."

"Are you on something?" Hazel said, aghast.

"Shut up. I know what I'm doing." Tatum looked at Dorinda with desperation in his eyes. "Remember when you came home early? Daddy on the bottom, white boy on the top? Daddy got busted. Remember?"

Dorinda maintained her silence. Hazel stood. She stared at Tatum, baffled.

"Look, I'm telling you, she can talk." Tatum's desperation turned to panic. "Please, Mama, say something. Please. You can talk. You know you can talk. You've been talking since I got here. Hazel doesn't believe it. You gotta show her. Hazel likes money. Hazel's full of shit."

"Fuck you," Hazel spat, then turned and stormed off.

Tatum stood and ran after Hazel. "Wait! Don't go. I'm telling you she can talk. She can talk. It was you. You did it. Your presence made her not want to talk. That's got to be it."

"What else could it be?" Hazel said as she headed back to the kitchen.

Tatum turned to see Dorinda, now facing his direction, smiling at him. She'd had her fun.

"Okey doke, okey doke." Bird whistles followed.

Tatum was livid. He ran over to Dorinda and snatched her by the collar as if he were dealing with a thug instead of his mother. "Why did you do that to me? You know you can talk. Quit clownin'."

Dorinda calmly turned her right hand palm up and moved her fingers, as if squeezing some imaginary object. Tatum then realized his close proximity to her and jumped back several feet. "You better maintain."

Tatum walked back to the kitchen where Hazel sat at the table waiting. He slumped down into his chair and looked straight ahead, confused, much like Dorinda. The kitchen was silent; the only sound was the television down the hall. Hazel stared at him. "I want to ask you something, and please don't get mad, okay? Just tell me. What drugs have you been doing? I know you like weed. But that shit you just pulled in there now was beyond weed."

Tatum didn't respond. He looked dazed.

"Look, we've got other issues to deal with, anyway," Hazel continued. "I think I just found a way to make us both some money. First of all, we lucked out with old girl having to leave that nursing home. That joint was eating up five grand a month as it was. When I was in Cali, I heard about a place there, where they take care of old people. It's a reconverted motel. It's not in the best part of town, but in her condition, what difference does it make? And it's only fifteen hundred a month. If we put her there, we can pocket the difference."

Tatum still seemed dazed, but he was listening.

"There's something else, too. Something even better. Somebody made us an offer on this place. It wasn't even on the market. It's just been sitting here. But some Indian dude saw it and inquired about it. He loves the house, and he's made of money. He wants to buy it for his two kids to live in while they study at the university. How'd you like to split four hundred thousand dollars? And the dude is ready. It's a done deal if we want it."

Tatum came out of his daze and looked at Hazel.

"Yeah, you heard right. 200K in your pocket, and you haven't even unpacked yet. The planets just lined up in our favor. We need to jump on this right now. We can take her to Cali in a couple days, drop her off, then come back and take care of the house. We basically flip 'em both at the same time. You can be out of Vegas and back in France where you belong, with more money than you've ever had in your whole life. So, what do you think of that, baby brother? Looks like you came back home and hit the jackpot."

Tatum smiled and offered his hand to his sister. The siblings shook hands to seal both the deal and their fate.

* * *

Tatum was gone, and Hazel was glad. He'd gotten on her nerves big time with his bullshit. Leave it to him to be away all those years, then show up giving orders—to her, of all people. The only thing that gives orders is balls, and Tatum was just like his daddy—a hot looking, cool talking dreamer who never amounted to anything. She couldn't wait to get his ass back to France, and she promised herself she'd personally drive him to the airport.

Hazel sat on the floor in one of the upstairs storage rooms. She'd already searched through several boxes, finding a variety of treasures. Beside her sat a crate of rare record albums. She was checking the eBay prices of the vinyl via her cellphone. So far, she was pleased by the results. Her phone rang, and she answered. "Hey, baby, lemme call you right back. I'm upstairs. I want to go back downstairs where I can relax and talk. I need to take a break, anyway."

Hazel ended the call. She stood, glanced around the room at the stacks of boxes surrounding her and smiled. Being stuck in the house was actually a good thing. It provided her the opportunity for extensive exploration. Those classic jazz albums were only the tip of the iceberg. Dorinda had an extensive collection of show business memorabilia as well.

There was gold hidden away within the mountains of boxes, and Hazel intended to do some serious prospecting.

Hazel exited the room and walked downstairs, indifferent to the pictures that hung on the wall. She walked into the living room, and like Tatum, her eyes were drawn to the moonlit grand piano. She walked over to the piano, and after a bit of inner debate, she seated herself. She warmed up with a few Hanon exercises, then launched into a Chopin etude, followed by a medley of boogie woogie tunes.

Hazel was a bit rusty, but still a far better player than Tatum. Named after Hazel Scott, the jazz pianist, she had been a child prodigy. Dorinda had recognized her skills early on and tried to force her onto a musical path. But Hazel hated the piano, regardless of her musical gifts. She resented her mother and rebelled and would forever be a disappointment in Dorinda's eyes.

Hazel stopped playing and massaged her fingers. Like Tatum, she hated this piano. She stood and headed to the kitchen. She took a bottle of beer from the refrigerator, seated herself, and placed her call.

"All right, I can talk now. I needed a break. I've been going through some stuff around here. There's a lot of money boxed up—more than I realized. Old girl was a pack rat, but she had good taste. Expensive tastes, too. No telling what all I'll find by the time I'm through." Hazel took a swig of beer as she listened. "No, he's gone, and he can stay gone, too. He just got here yesterday, and already he's out fruit loopin.' If he cared as much about getting his shit together as he did about getting his rocks off, he might add up to something more than zero. His idea of success is about how many twinks he can wreck in a night. He's useless."

As Hazel listened, she glanced around the kitchen in disgust. There were unwashed dishes in the sink and clutter on the countertop. The iron and several items of clothing lay on the ironing board where Tatum had haphazardly left them. There was even a stray bottle top on the floor lying beside the trash can. Tatum never changed. He always left a mess for somebody else to deal with, no matter how small.

"Yeah, I gave him the good news, all right. When I told him we'd split 400K for this joint, he lit up like a Christmas tree. He's an artist. He's an encyclopedia for stupid shit—who choreographed this, who designed that, blah, blah, blah. But he doesn't know shit about Zillow. Dumb ass." Hazel laughed. "If he knew how much this joint was really worth, there'd be a big brown stain in those purple leather pants. If I work it right, he'll be gone in a week for good." Hazel took another swig. "Yeah, sounds good. Call me when you get home, and we can talk later. Love you, too. Bye."

Hazel finished the last of her beer, then stood and stretched. The sound of the television down the hall caught her attention, and she decided to take a quick peek before going back upstairs. She walked down to the den and paused in the doorway. Dorinda sat facing the television, sitting in comfortable confusion as always.

Hazel scanned the room and saw nothing of value; certainly not her mother. The room was a bit brighter than normal. Besides the glow from the television, the bathroom light had been left on. Unlike Tatum, Hazel cared about such things. She had been paying the utility bills, not him. She entered the room, never even giving Dorinda a passing glance as she headed for the bathroom.

Hazel entered the bathroom, remembering the light switch wasn't on the wall but beside the mirror. Before turning off the light, she glanced at the various makeup items strewn across the sink and frowned. She debated whether to dump them in the trash now or later. But the sight of her own reflection in the mirror redirected her attention. Unlike Dorinda, who had always worn an overabundance of makeup, Hazel wore very little. She didn't need it. She took after her handsome father, who was born in New Orleans. With her fair skin, dark eyes, full lips, and mane of long, thick, curly hair, she looked like a Creole queen and knew it.

Hazel was a knockout, but she was growing bored with her current look. It was time for a new hairstyle; maybe something a bit more radical for a change. Maybe dreads. She'd never had them, and she had plenty of hair to work with. She toyed with her hair as she considered the possibilities. Like a sudden cool breeze, she felt the presence immediately, and it chilled her.

"Not this time."

Hazel was shocked by the voice. She turned and saw Dorinda standing in silhouette, a few steps from the doorway. It was unbelievable to see her up and out of the chair. And speaking? Hazel was paralyzed, as Dorinda moved closer, stepping out of the semi-darkness of the den and into the light of the doorway. Hazel had called her hideous when she'd first seen her. Now, standing in the bright light of the bathroom,

Dorinda looked demonic. What was she holding there?

"You're full of shit," Dorinda said, then lunged forward, swinging the iron full force into Hazel's jaw, shattering bone and ripping flesh. A red geyser erupted, spraying the walls and ceiling. The force of the blow sent Hazel spinning backward into the wall as blood and teeth spilled from the hole that had been her mouth. She bounced off the wall and collapsed to her knees.

Dorinda tossed the iron aside, then reached down, grabbed Hazel around the neck with both hands, and jerked her up to a standing position. She slammed Hazel back into the wall again and again while strangling her. Hazel tried to fight back, but Dorinda was too strong. Dorinda snatched Hazel by the hair and hurled her into the tub. She leaped in the tub, straddled Hazel, and seized her by the neck again. Dorinda then strangled the life out of what remained.

* * *

Tatum returned home a little after 3 A.M. Taking care not to make any noise, he entered as quietly as possible, as did his guest, Tyler. The floor lamp at the foot of the stairs was on, offering its paltry excuse for light. Tonight, the house seemed darker than usual. Tatum led the way upstairs, with Tyler following behind. The floor lamp below brought little light to the second floor, but it was sufficient. All four doors were closed. Tatum went first to Dorinda's room, furthest from the stairs. He eased open the door and peered inside. He could see the outlines of a figure beneath the bedspread. He closed the door.

Tatum proceeded to the clothing storage room and opened the door. He then remembered the mattresses were next door with all the boxes. Tyler lingered in the doorway, curious about the clothing hanging from the many racks. He wanted to explore but followed after Tatum, who led him to the next room. Tatum opened the door, turned on the light, and the two entered. Tatum noticed that many of the boxes had been opened and rummaged through, evidence of Hazel's active presence. He paid it no mind. He was more interested in the mattresses leaning against the wall. Tyler helped Tatum in laying one on the floor.

"Get comfortable. The bathroom is next door. I'm going downstairs to make something to eat."

Tatum walked out, closed the door behind him, and headed downstairs to the kitchen. He was already thinking about the various indignities he would unleash on young Tyler. It had been a while since he'd *rectified* a twink. Anybody with a gay porn name like Tyler Savage deserved to get rectified, and OG style, too. What should he use for a gag? Tatum's thoughts were making him weak with anticipation.

Upstairs, Tyler was still curious about those clothes next door. When it came to matters of fashion, he trusted his instincts. There was something fabulous to be found over there. He exited the room on tiptoe and went back to the clothing space. The door was slightly ajar. Tyler opened it and stepped inside, careful to close the door behind him. He turned on the light, and his eyes were immediately drawn to the first dress he encountered. Even through the clear protective covering, he could tell it was a special dress. He pulled down the zipper of the covering and removed the dress from its hanger—a long, red gown that shimmered in the light. It looked like a dress from the Golden Age of Hollywood.

Tyler stripped out of his clothes, tossed them on the floor, and slipped into the dress. It fit him perfectly, but he needed to see for himself. He exited the room and tiptoed barefoot to the bathroom, closing the door behind him. He turned on the light and looked at his reflection in the mirror above the sink. The dress looked good on him, all right, and he was delighted by the sight. Tyler undid the bun in his blonde hair, allowing his long locks to fall freely about his shoulders. Now he looked gorgeous—even better than a movie star. What would Tatum think? Would he be overcome with lust? Would he fall madly in love? It was time to find out.

Tyler stepped out of the bathroom and saw Dorinda standing in the doorway of her bedroom. He was stunned by the sight of her, along with her made-up face, and her white gown stained with dried blood. Dorinda was stunned as well. The sight of Tyler wearing her dress sparked a crazed rage in her. There was murder in her eyes. She advanced toward him.

"Tatum?" Tyler spoke the name, but it was barely a whisper, he was so scared. "Tatum?" The voice was louder now, and with more fear, but still could not be heard downstairs.

Dorinda rushed at him at the moment he screamed, and

silenced him. She snatched him by the hair with one hand and covered his mouth with her other, sticking fingers down his throat and gagging him. She twisted his head as if determined to rip it from his shoulders.

Tyler struggled against her, but she was too strong, slinging him to and fro like a rag doll. Dorinda dragged him back into the bathroom, raised the toilet seat with her foot, and slammed his head into the porcelain again and again. She twisted his arms behind him, forced his face down into the toilet water and held him there as he struggled desperately for his life, even as it was slipping away from him. Dorinda kept his face submerged long after he stopped moving.

Downstairs, Tatum was oblivious to the violent spectacle taking place upstairs. He was busy preparing a food tray while he entertained thoughts of the perversions to come. The sound of the television down the hall redirected his attention. He assumed Dorinda was in her upstairs bedroom. Perhaps Hazel was now in the den, still awake and watching television. Perhaps she'd fallen asleep and left the television on. He decided to find out.

Tatum walked down the hallway and entered the den. Dorinda's chair sat empty, facing the glowing television. The bed was empty, as well, and hadn't been slept in. The bathroom door was ajar, and the light was on.

"Hazel? I'm back."

There was no answer. Tatum walked over to the bathroom door and knocked, causing the door to swing open. He gasped at the blood on the walls. He stepped inside and looked toward the bathtub with its drawn shower curtain. He slowly pulled back the curtain and found the tub empty.

The piano music startled him. And frightened him. He recognized Dorinda's playing. The music was forceful and loud enough to be heard in this part of the house. He even recognized the tune. It was the old song, *We're in the Money*, one of her favorites, only this version was faster and more frenzied than normal.

Tatum walked out of the bathroom and back to the kitchen. Now, the music was near deafening, laden with rage. Dorinda played as if she were attacking the instrument, or perhaps rather using the music to attack the listener.

Tatum walked out of the brightness of the kitchen and entered the moonlit living room. He beheld Dorinda seated at the piano in all her horrific glory, looking like an apparition. She appeared to be in a trance as she swayed back and forth, pounding the keyboard with fury and abandon. As Tatum approached, she didn't seem to notice him. Positioned beside the piano were a chair and loveseat. They had been moved from their regular spots in the room and brought closer to the piano, facing it. There were guests in the seats, but Tatum could only see them from behind.

Tatum came closer to Dorinda, close enough to see her blood-stained gown and hands. She was grinning from ear-to-ear but appeared out of her head and unaware of his presence. Tatum now had a better vantage point with which to see the seated guests. Tyler was seated in the chair, dressed in red. His face was battered, his eyes were open, and his mouth hung slack, as if frozen in mid scream. Oddly, his legs were crossed, and his hands were folded in his lap. But there was no life in him. Hazel sat in the loveseat. Her eyes were open, and the bottom half of her face was an unrecognizable pulp.

Tatum turned to run, but Dorinda sprung up from the bench and leaped onto his back, dragging him to the floor. She held fast to him as he crawled crab-like out of the living room into the light of the foyer. She clawed at him, hissing like a beast. Tatum managed to push her away long enough to get to his feet. He ran to the front door and struggled to unlock it.

Dorinda was on her feet. She grabbed the floor lamp and, using it like a club, swung the base into Tatum's head, and he fell at her feet. The lamp cord was ripped from the wall and the foyer went dark. As Tatum lay dazed and spasming on the floor, Dorinda slammed the base of the lamp down onto his head repeatedly, as if churning butter. When he stopped moving, she tossed the lamp aside, grabbed him by the collar, and dragged him back into the living room.

Dorinda appeared to be fortified by the violence of the evening. She hurled Tatum into the loveseat beside Hazel. The two lifeless siblings leaned on each other, head-to-head. Dorinda repositioned them so they sat upright, even taking the time to cross their legs as she'd done with Tyler. Once they appeared more presentable, she returned to her piano and sat down.

Now that all the guests were properly seated, Dorinda

was ready to perform. She smiled as she played her favorite song; a song she'd loved since childhood.

Lulu's Back in Town.

* * *

Reuben sounded secure in the knowledge his latest tale had made a positive impact. "So that's Dorinda. I think this story is less moody and more direct than the one before. The violence is a lot more upfront, that's for sure. I'd call it a character-driven, family-focused horror story."

Jill glanced down at the detailed notecards lying atop the closed briefcase. Reuben had worked his magic yet again, and she'd captured it all. This new story proved to be as entertaining as the last, if not more so. She wondered how best to conceal her true feelings this time. Fortunately, Reuben continued with his commentary, buying her more time to think.

"This is actually more of a traditional style Grand Guignol story. It's not supernatural at all. Traditional Grand Guignol tends to avoid supernatural elements. The stories are more grounded in realism. Real life is every bit as spooky as the supernatural. Maybe even more so. After all, real life is, well… *real.* So, there it is. What do you think?

Jill loved the story, of course, but she wasn't about to let Reuben know that. He was a fount of magical ideas, and she certainly didn't want to block the flow, which she'd nearly done after her last critique. What was needed now was a completely different tactic. Rather than discourage him with overt criticism, she'd encourage him with stealthful compliments, seasoned with subterfuge.

"That's a great story, Reuben. A nice, tight, little plot, great characters. Dorinda is plenty scary, all right. And like you said, the story is totally grounded in reality. It's a little long—longer than the other story. But that's okay because it makes for a slow burn. And the ending delivers big time. I love it."

"Well, that's good to hear." Reuben sounded relieved.

"But when I hear good stories, the producer in me immediately thinks about the audience. I'm just concerned about the general public, that's all."

"What do you mean?"

"You said the story is traditional Grand Guignol which doesn't really get into the supernatural. That could be problematic."

"How so?"

"Well, modern audiences tend to actually *like* supernatural elements. Like monsters. Monsters never go out of style. Everybody loves them—especially the kids. In fact, if you think about it, we're due for a new monster right now. Overdue, really. The modern world needs a new horror icon. Who was the last great one, anyway? Hard to even say, they're so few and far between these days. Maybe Jigsaw from the *Saw* franchise. He's okay, but he's pretty weak next to something like Pinhead. Pinhead was the last really great one, and he's from the 80s. Do you have any stories with a good monster?"

"As a matter of fact, I do."

Gina

Braxton Morello stood behind the counter of his empty store—empty of customers, that is. The store itself was filled with goodies galore. One corner of the store was devoted entirely to comic books. The opposite corner featured DVDs, specializing in horror, sci-fi, and fantasy films. One entire wall displayed fantasy figurines and monster toys. The rest of the wall space was plastered with posters. In the middle of the store was a maze of shelves filled with books. Punk rock provided the musical soundtrack. Braxton's store was both eclectic and cool. It had everything except customers. So unfortunately, it was a cool tomb. Braxton checked his watch. It was 8:45 P.M. He looked around the store and sighed.

A teenage girl entered with a skateboard under one arm and a psychedelic satchel slung over her shoulder. She was a tomboy, gypsy princess, dressed in a funky mix of leather and Levi, accented with brightly colored scarves and combat boots adorned with charms. Her head was crowned with an enormous multi-colored Rasta beanie. Her name was Zana.

"What's up, Mister B?" Zana asked.

Braxton's dark mood lightened. He looked at his watch with concern. "It's a little late, isn't it?"

Zana placed her skateboard on the floor and leaned it against the counter. She and Braxton slapped palms, then locked their little fingers together in their special greeting between friends.

"I'm on my way home now. Just passin' through. Thought I'd drop by. Everything all right?"

Braxton watched Zana scan the nooks and crannies of his empty store, searching for customers. He sensed her concern and addressed it with a touch of cynicism. "It wasn't too bad today. I actually sold a comic this afternoon."

Zana danced over to the DVD corner to check out the martial arts section. "Stay up, Mister B. This is the coolest store in Vegas. It's just a matter of time before people find out about it. I tell everybody I know. Maybe I should make some flyers and spread them around. I could put them up at bus stops and supermarkets. I don't know why I never thought of that. I should do that. First thing tomorrow I'm—"

"No, you shouldn't. I'm okay. Everything is fine."

"It's just not right this place is empty. People should know about it."

Braxton looked around his store with a wistful smile. "I'm just in the wrong place at the wrong time. Sure looks like it, doesn't it? I always dreamed of having a place just like this. Well, here it is. My place. My *space.*" He laughed at his choice of words. "More people are going to Myspace than coming here."

"This place rocks. You built something to be proud of."

"Unfortunately, the world changed while I was building it. People don't need a tactile, hands on, physical shopping experience—not anymore. They'd rather get it online. They'll probably get it cheaper, anyway. And nobody needs the physical interaction with other human beings that you get in a place like this. Where you come in to buy something, get involved in a discussion—or even a debate—and end up making a friend. These days, you make your friends online, too. You can hang out with the whole world at home on your phone."

Zana couldn't argue with the truth, but she tried anyway. "All I know is that I feel something special whenever I come in here. I don't get that feeling anywhere else. I don't even get that at home."

Braxton shot a glance at Zana. He'd always wondered if she were homeless. He probed. "Speaking of home, I'm going to be closing this pop stand in a minute. It's absolutely no problem for me to drop you off. Where do you live, anyway?"

Zana didn't answer. She was too absorbed by the text of the Donnie Yen DVD she was reading—or so it seemed. She redirected the conversation. "There's nothing like your place anywhere in Vegas. You've got all the right stuff, the cool stuff. But it's more than that. Your place is more than just the merchandise. It's just like you said. You come in here to buy something and end up making a friend. That's magic. That's what happened the first time I came in. Remember?"

"Sure do."

"That doesn't happen at Walmart … or anywhere else, for that matter. We need places like this. This place is the last of something that we need to be holding onto. I'd rather be here than anywhere."

"You're a sweet pea, but I think that maybe you're in the wrong place at the wrong time, too. You and I both. We're the only people who seem to care about my crazy dream. I built the perfect spot twenty years too late."

"It's gonna turn around for you, Mister B. I can feel it. But you've got to stay up. No matter what happens, you've gotta stay up." Zana's plea was heartfelt and endearing. Her eyes remained fixed on the DVD she'd been holding.

A large group of Asian tourists suddenly stormed into the store like a thundering herd and scattered in all directions. They seemed excited to have found such a place. Braxton was more excited they'd found it. Zana focused on her DVD and pretended not to notice the small crowd, but she was more excited than Braxton.

"If anyone needs any help, just let me know," Braxton called out.

The tourists didn't seem to hear Braxton. They were all too engrossed in their tactile, hands-on, physical shopping experience. Their enthusiasm filled the store with positive energy, and Braxton looked happy and hopeful. Sometimes, right at closing time, a patron can enter a business and singlehandedly make up for a disastrous day, or even a disastrous week. This looked to be one of those occasions. Zana still pretended not to notice.

The door opened again, and an Asian man peered inside

the store. He spoke to the tourists in either Mandarin or Cantonese. The dialect didn't matter, but the response certainly did. Every single tourist simultaneously stopped what they were doing, dropped what they were holding, and exited the store *en masse* as if running late for the last available flight. Braxton watched in stunned disbelief as the last of them left. Perhaps some nearby buffet was closing soon.

As Braxton stared at the entrance door, he didn't notice that Zana had worked her way throughout the store, picking up various items for purchase. Moments later, she approached and placed a DVD, a hardback book, and several comic books on the counter. Rather than look Braxton in the eye, Zana feigned interest in a colorful counter display of superhero keychains. Braxton wasn't going for it.

"Bullshit," he said. "This is a pity purchase. Just like last week. It's getting to be a habit, too. I'm not as dumb as I apparently must look. Put it back. All of it."

"I need this stuff." Zana seemed shocked by the insinuation. "I know what I need."

"I know I don't believe you. So put it back."

"No. Besides, I'm a big girl. I do whatever I want with my money. I got money."

Zana removed her wallet from her back pocket, peered inside, and saw a total of three dollars. Braxton pretended not to have noticed.

"I'll be right back," she said. Zana kept her eyes averted.

"Where are you going?"

"I just need to make a quick run. I'll be right back."

"Put it back, Zana. I don't want to argue about this."

"Then stop arguing. The only person trippin' is you. I'll be right back."

Braxton could see that he wasn't going to win this fight, so he softened a bit. "Look, if you really want this stuff, I can just hold it. I got a better idea, anyway. You know what? Just take it with you and pay me when I see you again. You're in here all the time, anyway. You'll probably be back tomorrow. There's no reason for you to come back tonight. It doesn't make any—"

"Look, I got money. I just don't have it on me, that's all. I'll be right back." Her tone was defiant.

"This is stupid."

"I'm not nearly as broke as I apparently look. What do you think I am, anyway—homeless?" She removed a watch from her jeans. It was an old school pocket watch attached to a chain, something more fitting for a grandfather than a teenager. She opened it. "It's almost time for you to close. I'll be back before you close."

Zana grabbed her skateboard, which she'd left propped against the counter. She hurried out of the store before Braxton could say another word in protest. He watched her exit and wondered again about her housing arrangements. He opened the cash register, which was empty except for a few singles, and blew out imaginary dust. "We'll try again tomorrow," he said out loud. "I believe we're done for this evening."

Braxton took a shopping bag from beneath the counter

and placed Zana's items inside. The entrance door opened, and three men entered. They were white men dressed in black suits, with an aura of uncool authority. One of them, who appeared to be the leader, walked up to the counter flanked by his two associates.

"Good evening. My name is Chalmers," he said. "These are my associates, Reynolds and Daniels."

"Good evening. May I help you?" Ordinarily, Braxton would have been elated by three potential customers after a day of no business. Not tonight. These men looked like trouble.

Chalmers glanced around the store with admiration. His two associates stared straight ahead, focused on Braxton. "Nice place you have here. It's been what... almost a year now? Most new businesses in Las Vegas don't last that long, especially these days. You should be proud."

"You know, I actually close at nine. May I help you?"

"Running a fanboy store is a far cry from your old life. This could hardly be considered a step up... Doctor Morello."

Braxton was surprised to be addressed as a doctor. Now he looked at the men with suspicion, as he tried to hide his unease. He didn't answer. He wasn't sure what to say.

"It's clear that you're on the downlow, as they say, doctor. Not to worry. Your secret is safe with us. All we want is a word with you. That's all we want."

Braxton was determined to appear nonchalant in the face of his growing anxiety. He tried false bravado. "So which alphabet club do you guys belong to? I've paid my taxes, so you're not IRS. CIA? NSA? KGB? You're too old to be Mormon missionaries. Girl Scouts? Who are you and what do you want from me?"

Chalmers laughed. His associates remained stone-faced. "Doctor Braxton Morello. Your work in biotechnology, genetics, and genomics is legendary. Your vast achievements can be found in university textbooks all over the world. In the scientific community, you're a bonafide rock star."

"That's right. I'm the Hendrix of genetic engineering. I'm experienced. So what? I hung up my Strat a long time ago."

"It hasn't been that long, Doctor. I'm curious, why did you leave the scientific stage?"

"Why? Because the gig got out of hand, that's why. Way out of hand. I got involved in things I should have left alone. I prefer this gig. It's a lot less complicated. Safer, too."

Chalmers smiled like a cobra. "Doctor Morello, you're much too talented to be wasting your time here, selling comics and trinkets and making no money at it. You could be putting your considerable skills to much better use. For society. For your country."

Braxton burst into laughter and made no effort to hide his contempt. "So, you *are* the Man. You must be that rogue element I've heard so much about. Did you find a parking space for your black helicopter? I thought you guys were just a figment of Alex Jones's imagination."

Chalmers stopped smiling and stared at Braxton with ice in his eyes. His words were even more chilling. "We're aware that certain units in this complex have underground chambers, and this unit is one of them. There's something going on around here, Doctor Morello. Something beyond comics and trinkets." Chalmers pointed toward the floor. "And it's going on down there. Before we leave here tonight, we're going to find out exactly what it is. And what's more, Doctor Morello, you're going to do your patriotic duty and work with us."

"Work with you?" Braxton's bravado was fading. "What do you want from me? I'm just a scientist."

"Your expertise would be of invaluable…"

"You can't force me to do anything! I haven't committed any crime, so you can't turn me. You've got nothing on me. You understand that? So, kiss my ass, man in black."

Reynolds handed Chalmers an iPad. Chalmers held it to where Braxton could see it. "Take a peek at this, Doctor Morello. Do you remember your colleague, Doctor Shevchenko? He had some reservations, too." Chalmers activated a video, filling the store with the sounds of sobbing and pleading.

Braxton looked at the screen and was horrified by the sight. He looked away. A long tortuous scream was more than he could bear. "Turn it off!"

Chalmers handed the iPad back to Reynolds. "Unfortunately, we were unable to reason with him. Hopefully, we'll have better luck with you." Chalmers indicated a door behind Braxton. "That door there. Where does it lead?"

Braxton braced himself against the counter, the only thing separating him from these men. "It's for storage."

"Let's take a look."

The three men walked around the counter, but Braxton confronted them, blocking them from moving further. "I don't think so."

Reynolds slammed his palm into Braxton's chest, and the force knocked him back into a wall. Dazed, he slid to the floor with the wind knocked out of him.

"We don't care what you think, Doctor Morello," said Chalmers. He stepped over Braxton and opened the door, followed by his associates. The three men entered a storage room. The walls were stocked with store merchandise. Across the room was another door, and Chalmers smiled when he saw it. The three men walked toward the door, but Braxton rushed in and positioned himself in front of them.

"This is my place! You can't just come in here and—"

"We've been watching you for some time. There's something going on here, Doctor Morello. And tonight, we're going to find out exactly what it is." Chalmers pointed to the door. "Where does that lead?"

"I'm calling the police!"

Chalmers looked pleased by the suggestion. "Da do do do, De dah dah dah," he sang. His associates laughed. Chalmers removed a cellphone from his jacket and offered it to Braxton. "That's a great idea. Go ahead. Call the police. They can join us, and we can all explore together. The more, the merrier."

Braxton stared at the phone, as he reflected on Chalmer's words.

"You don't really want the police here, now do you,

Doctor Morello? Besides, the police don't work for you, they work for us. Now, I believe it's time you gave us a tour of the facilities, don't you think? The *real* facilities. Let's go."

Braxton looked like a trapped animal. Resigned to his fate, he led the men over to the door.

"So exactly where are we going, Doctor Morello?"

"Where do you think, asshole? Frankenstein's laboratory."

Braxton opened the door and led the men down a narrow spiral staircase to another door. He opened the door, turned on a light, and led the men into his laboratory. There were several floor-to-ceiling bookshelves bulging with books. The available wall space was covered with enormous, detailed images of the human anatomy, the sole exception being a poster of Jimi Hendrix. In the middle of the room was a long table covered with the tools of science. There were test tubes filled with colored liquids, beakers, Bunsen burners, and an unusually large microscope. The end of the table was blanketed with open books.

"Quite impressive, Doctor Morello. I expected no less."

Braxton looked as if he'd been violated, and Chalmers enjoyed the intrusion. In a far corner was a gigantic upright freezer, like something from a meatpacking plant. Beside the freezer was a massive steel door. Chalmers was intrigued. He walked over to the freezer, followed by his associates. Braxton hurried after them. Chalmers opened the freezer and found it filled with huge slabs of meat hanging from hooks. He looked perplexed.

"What's going on here?"

"I'm not a vegetarian."

"I can see that."

Chalmers turned his focus to the steel door. It looked like a door to a bank vault. Mounted on the wall beside the door was an intercom system.

"That's quite an unusual door, Doctor Morello. Let me guess—more storage?"

"Uh… it was here already. This place used to be a jewelry store. They probably kept the rare stuff in there. I just use it for storage."

Chalmers didn't buy the explanation. "Doctor Morello, I have a unique gift. I suppose you could call it a kind of radar. It serves me well in my profession. When I'm close to something of significance, my radar lets me know. And it's never failed me yet." Chalmers glanced around the laboratory. "From the looks of this place, you never hung up your Strat, Doctor Morello. Clearly, you're still rockin.' You've put out a lot of product in your life, but my radar tells me your biggest hit is right behind this door."

Chalmers advanced, but Braxton pushed him back into his associates and positioned himself in front of the door. His fear was now replaced by rage.

"Enough of your bully bullshit. Get out of here!"

Reynolds and Daniels rushed forward. Reynolds punched Braxton in the face, and the blow dropped him to his knees. Daniels snatched him by the collar and lifted him off the floor, allowing Reynolds to punch him in the gut. Daniels then slammed Braxton to the floor, and he lay in a dazed pile as blood trickled from his mouth. He struggled to catch his breath. Daniels was about to kick him.

"Leave him alone!"

The three men turned simultaneously and witnessed Zana rushing toward them, wielding a wooden chair. She swung the chair full force, and it connected with Daniel's head, shattering completely, and he collapsed. Zana dived to the floor, then rolled back to her feet with a set of spinning nunchucks in hand. She attacked Chalmers and Reynolds, raining blows on them both with painful accuracy. She had them on the defensive until a revived Daniels grabbed her hair from behind and slammed her to the floor. He stomped her like a bug.

Braxton had a clear view of the savage proceedings, and his body spasmed with each attack. "Stop! Don't hurt her!"

Chalmers looked down at the half-conscious Zana, and his eyes reflected darkness and perversion. "I've got big plans for you, little lady—later."

A beeping sound from the intercom system beside the steel door shifted everyone's attention. A small red bulb on the control panel flashed, and a voice was heard, distinctly female, almost child-like in its sweetness and innocence.

"Braxton? What's going on out there?" asked the voice. She sounded fearful. "Are you all right? What's all that noise?"

"Who is that in there?" Asked Chalmers.

Braxton was hurt from the beating. He lay on the floor, his concerned eyes focused on Zana, who lay nearby. "She's my patient. She's in quarantine. Just leave her out of this. Leave her alone. Please."

Braxton managed to crawl over to Zana. He cradled her in his arms.

The red bulb on the intercom flashed again. "Braxton? Please say something. What's going on out there. Are you all right? I'm afraid." The voice sounded more alarmed.

Chalmers looked at the door, then down at Braxton. "Storage indeed. I think it's time we have a look at whoever it is you've got in storage." Chalmers motioned toward the door. "Reynolds, go take a look."

"Please. Leave her alone!" Yelled Braxton.

The red bulb flashed again. "Braxton? I'm afraid."

Reynolds walked over to the door. There was no knob or latch, but rather a large, round steering column attached. Reynolds took hold and rotated it until there was an audible "click." He pulled the door open and entered. The door swung back of its own accord, closing completely with a "click."

"I've had enough of you, Doctor Morello." Chalmers was still furious. "You've spent a little too much time in the lab. You don't understand reality. But you're going to get a crash course this evening. You and your little dragon here."

Gut-wrenching, agonized male screams from inside the storage vault startled everyone.

"Reynolds? Reynolds?" Chalmers shouted loud enough to be heard. "What's going on in there? Daniels, go take a look."

Daniel's eyes were fixed on the storage vault door.

Chalmers repeated, but with more irritation. "I said 'go take a look!'"

Daniels complied, but with hesitation. He walked over to the door, rotated the wheel, and entered. When the door closed behind him, it didn't "click," and Braxton's mood lightened considerably. He burst into laughter, and Chalmers looked at him confused.

"What's going on here, Doctor Morello?"

Braxton looked up at Chalmers while holding Zana in his arms. "Do you know what a transgenic is, sphincter face? You're about to. You're about to meet my foxy lady."

There was another scream, more intense and unsettling than the one before. The vault door swung open, and Daniels emerged, but he wasn't walking. He was being carried, held by his hair, suspended with his feet dangling. His body blocked the view of whoever was carrying him.

Though still on the floor, Braxton had more strength now. He grabbed hold of the fallen Zana and pulled her over to a nearby bookshelf. He propped her up into a seated position and wiped her brow. She was fully conscious now. Both she and Braxton had a clear view of the unfolding events, as did Chalmers. All eyes were now on Daniels, dangling before them.

Daniels was hurled to the ground, and Gina was revealed in all her terrifying glory. She stood over seven feet tall. Her face was a living skull with deep, sunken eye sockets, a gaping hole where a nose should have been, and a fanged tooth mouth dripping with blood. Her head was crowned by a thick mane of wild, red hair that hung past her shoulders. A long serpentine tongue darted from her mouth. Her arms were long, thick, muscular, and covered with hair. Instead of hands, she had huge, sectioned claws. Her breasts were large, and she had six of them, three pairs running in parallel down her belly. Her legs were like her arms—thick, muscled, and hairy. Instead of feet or even claws, she had cloven hooves. She had the tail of a scorpion, and it extended up her back and curled over the top of her head. At the end of the tail was a rattler. Gina was a living nightmare, and Chalmers trembled at the sight of her.

Braxton wasn't afraid. He looked at Gina with adoration. Gina was more than just his greatest scientific masterpiece. She was the love of his life, and it showed in his eyes. "Hey, baby, you okay?"

"What's going on, Braxton? Who are these men? I'm afraid." Gina's soft, sweet voice was filled with affection and concern, a bizarre contrast to her hideous appearance.

"Don't be scared, baby," Braxton reassured her. "Everything is going to be okay now."

"Who are these men? Why are they here? Why are you on the floor? Did they hurt you?"

"Yes, Gina, they hurt me."

Gina growled like a beast and focused her gaze on Daniels, who lay on the floor, stretched out before her, too paralyzed to move. She threw herself on top of him, straddled him, and proceeded to feed, starting first with his face. Chalmers stood nearby, horrified by the sight of the struggling Daniels being eaten alive.

Braxton watched Gina with smiling admiration, much like a proud parent. "She's something, isn't she? But I went a bit too far. You can see that." He laughed.

Chalmers had seen enough. He bolted, heading for the exit door. Zana stuck out her leg, tripping him, and he stumbled and fell to the floor. Braxton had regained his strength. He stood and walked toward Chalmers.

"You told me I was going to get a crash course in reality tonight. Isn't that what you said, man in black?" Braxton followed the question with a kick to Chalmer's head, and the force sent him rolling. Braxton snatched him by the hair, stood him up on wobbly legs, and pointed over to Gina, who continued to feed on Daniels. "Now *that's* reality!" He laughed. "It's alive! It's alive!"

Zana was on her feet now. She rushed over to where the men stood and punched Chalmers in the stomach. He doubled over, but Braxton held him firm to keep him from collapsing. She punched him again.

"Gina? Baby, you want some more?" Braxton sounded as if he were offering ice cream to a child.

Gina looked up from her still quivering meal, as blood and flesh spilled from her gaping maw. She wanted more. Working as a team, Braxton and Zana both flung Chalmers toward Gina. With lightning quick reflexes, Gina stood and snatched Chalmers by the throat with one of her massive claws. Her long, thick tail moved down her back, curling its way between her legs, slowly thrusting outward. The rattler at the end moved excitedly, and the reptilian-like outer skin slid back revealing moist, pink flesh. Gina's tail wasn't a tail at all, and it appeared to be quite aroused. Gina's appendage thrust its way up and into Chalmers body, lifting him completely off the ground. Impaled, Chalmers dangled on the end of Gina, as she moved him up and down, side to side.

Braxton took Zana by the hand, and they walked over to the laboratory door. "Let's give them some quality time together. We've got a lot to talk about, anyway."

When they reached the door, Zana turned back to witness Gina pinning Chalmers to the wall as he screamed and struggled. "Wow, she's amazing."

Braxton hugged Zana. "And so are you. My two favorite girls in the whole wide world."

Braxton kissed Zana's forehead, and they walked out of the laboratory, closing the door behind them.

* * *

Jill's eyes were glazed. Fresh, detailed notecards filled with Gina's tale lay on top of her briefcase beside her. She flipped through a couple of pages of her notebook that now contained various drawings of Gina in all her terrifying glory. Jill was a gifted artist who drew as well as she lied. Once again, Jill had absorbed Reuben's magical ideas with merciless expertise.

"Gina is a monster, and there are horrific elements to the story—like the ending," said Reuben. "But it's really more of a comedy. That's *very* Grand Guignol, by the way. Comedy was a big part of the Grand Guignol experience. There would be one or two crazy plays, then they'd throw a comedy at you. Then they'd do something crazy again."

Jill collected her thoughts as she constructed a response. Reuben had deftly reinvented Mary Shelley's classic story for a modern audience. Now, Dr. Frankenstein was a quirky genetic scientist running a fanboy store with a monster in the basement. Jill had written the name Nic Cage on the first notecard. Gina was a monster with a twist. She looked like a demon yet had the demeanor of an angel. The basic concept made for a mashup that was both crazy and compelling. Once again, Reuben had worked his magic. Jill stared at her own artwork. She had visually captured Gina with astonishing perfection. Jill was now looking at the next iconic monster, and she knew it. Reuben had outdone himself, and he knew it.

"So that's Gina. Is she iconic enough for you?"

As Reuben awaited a response, Jill eased back into character. The game of deception is tricky, akin to walking a tightrope, and coolness is crucial. Jill was glacial. "That was a great story, Reuben. I really liked that one, too. You did it again. And yeah, Gina is definitely off the chain." Jill wasn't exactly turning backflips with excitement.

"Off the chain? Just off the chain?" Reuben's radar picked up on Jill's distinct lack of enthusiasm, and now, his disappointment was turning to annoyance. "Gina is one of the most original monsters of all time. I'd put her up against anybody. Even Pinhead."

Jill sensed the irritation in Reuben's voice and proceeded carefully. "I loved it, Reuben. Really, I did. It's just... I don't know. First of all, you've got a monster unlike anything we've ever seen before. It's more unique than derivative. Way more unique. Maybe the ratio between unique and derivative is too unbalanced, and that's the problem. You've got to remember, when it comes to monsters, people can be conservative. People tend to like variations of what they already know. Vampires, werewolves, zombies, masked maniacs, lawyers, and politicians—the usual suspects. Pre-awareness is everything, especially these days."

Reuben pleaded his defense. "But the pre-awareness is right there. That's why she's so perfect. Gina is a transgenic—the modern-day equivalent of a Frankenstein's monster. The Frankenstein monster was made of different dead bodies. Gina is made of different species. Same thing, but totally different. That's uniquely derivative, isn't it?"

Reuben was quite right, and Jill was unable to come up with a suitable rebuttal. "Uh… yes, it is. Don't get me wrong, Reuben, Gina is a great monster. She's wonderful."

"So, what's the problem?"

"I understand that she's a modern Frankenstein's monster. I just think your take on the monster is less traditional and more… I don't know… avant garde maybe? Gina is pretty out there, that's for sure. Maybe too much so. She's so different that she might just sail over the heads of the very people you want to reach. And there's something else you need to keep in mind. Something very important. The whole thing of Gina being female might be problematic. It could prove to be a tough sell. I know it's sexist, but people tend to prefer male monsters. That's just the sad reality. How many iconic female monsters can you even name?" Jill could name a few but declined to mention them.

Reuben fell silent and argued no further. Jill was a nimble performer on her tightrope of deception. She wasn't about to leave his morale shattered. Quite the contrary.

"That was a great story, Reuben. I loved it. And Gina

really is iconic. It's a brilliant concept. I just think it's too brilliant for today's audience, that's all. You may just be ahead of your time on this one. What about ghost stories? Do you have any ghost stories? I'd love to hear what you'd do with one of those."

"I've got a ghost story. I don't know how scary it is, though. I'm not sure it's scary at all."

"I don't care, Reuben. There're only two kinds of stories, anyway—good ones and bad ones. Let me hear it. I can hardly wait."

"Well, here's a ghostly encounter—with a Terminator twist."

Roland Phoenix

The motel was called The Phoenix. It was a one-story motel with eighteen units, built sometime during the glory days of Las Vegas. It was shaped like a horseshoe, with a small parking lot in the middle area surrounded by apartment units, with an office next to the first unit. A neon sign hanging in the office window said "Open," even though the motel itself looked closed. More than closed, it looked condemned or needed to be.

The Phoenix had no doubt been a scandalous hot spot back in the day, but now, it was a retro eyesore, barely a shadow of its former self. Indeed, with the ongoing beautification and rejuvenation projects taking place up and down Fremont Street in recent years, The Phoenix was surely destined for demolition. Yet there it stood—at least for now.

It was after midnight when a late model sedan pulled into the empty parking lot. A man in a trench coat and fedora stepped out. Roland Griffin removed a suitcase from the backseat, then made his way to the office. The bright neon lights of Glitter Gulch glowed far in the distance. This end of Fremont Street was considerably darker.

Roland entered the office. Unlike the motel's exterior, the office was well maintained. In the corner was a lounge area with a comfortable couch. Nearby stood a well-stocked vending machine. A television hung from the ceiling. It was turned off. An unseen stereo played Tony Bennett.

A man behind the service counter who looked to be in his eighties, was dressed in a gray, flannel suit and red tie. He had a chiseled, weather-worn face with deep wrinkles. His long, white hair hung down past his shoulders. Whatever his ethnicity, there was Native American in the mix. His name was Leo. He was pleasantly surprised to have a guest tonight.

"Welcome to The Phoenix. It's a pleasure to have you with us."

Roland walked over to the counter and placed his suitcase on the floor. There were two barstools at the counter, but Roland remained standing. Leo slid the registration book closer to Roland.

"Thanks." Roland signed his name. "I wasn't sure if this place was even open."

Leo laughed. "Well, it is, and it isn't. I mean, we're open, but no one comes here much anymore. It's not as nice as some of the other places around here. But it's clean, I can promise you that. How long will you be staying with us Mister…" Leo glanced down at the name in the registration book. "Griffin?"

"Just overnight."

"Overnight? In Las Vegas? You're not going to stick around long enough to donate to one of our many local charities?"

"You mean like Feed the Casinos? Or Save the Strippers? Not this time. I'm a little long in the tooth for that stuff, anyway. No, I'm going home tomorrow."

"Where's home?"

"I'm from Ohio. I drove out to Arizona last week. Every year, I get together with some of the guys I served with—the ones who are left, anyway. We get together, eat good food, make a toast… cry a little. It's a tradition. Been doing it for years. Do you need my credit card to—"

"Nope. Just pay when you leave." Leo removed one of the keys hanging on the wall behind him. "Follow me, and I'll show you to your room."

Leo came from behind the counter and picked up Roland's suitcase. The two men exited the office, with Leo leading the way. Leo led Roland to the door of unit number one, next to the office. He opened the door, and the two men entered.

Like the office, the room bore little resemblance to the exterior of the motel. It was clean and well maintained. There were two twin beds, one near the door, one on the opposite side of the room. There was a dresser against the wall, beneath a television suspended from the ceiling. Leo sat the suitcase down and handed the room key to Roland. He went across the room to the bathroom, opened the door, and turned on the light. The bathroom was small but clean. Directly opposite the bathroom door was a door frame built into the wall.

"There should be plenty of towels. And there's more soap under the sink if you need it."

"Thanks. I appreciate it."

Leo walked back over to the entrance door. "So, you're all set. The office is open twenty-four hours. So, if you need anything, you just call me." Leo pointed at the phone on the nightstand beside one of the beds. "I'm the only one, but I'm always here." Leo extended his hand. "Have a good sleep, Mister Griffin. Very nice to have you with us tonight."

Roland shook Leo's hand and closed the door behind him. He hung his hat and trench coat in the closet and placed his suitcase on top of the dresser. He kicked off his shoes and plopped down on the bed closest to the door.

There was a remote control on the nightstand beside the phone. Roland turned on the television and channel surfed. There was nothing he wanted to see, but he left the television on low. It provided a bit of light. Roland had barely lowered his head onto the pillow before he was fast asleep.

* * *

Roland was awakened by the sound of knocking. It was soft but loud enough to be heard. But where was it coming from? Roland sat up, glanced at the entrance door, and listened. Silence. Had he dreamt it? More knocks soon dismissed that notion, but they weren't coming from outside his room. They were coming from inside the bathroom. Roland stood, confused. It made no sense. The bathroom door eased open, and a small face peered out into view. It was a young girl, perhaps eight years old.

"Mister, I'm sorry to bother you."

Roland didn't answer but only stared at her.

"Can I watch your TV? They won't let me watch what I want to watch over there. I want to see my movie. Can I watch it over here? Please?"

Roland nodded, reflexively. There was no reason to say no. The sweet sincerity of her plea overcame any reluctance he might have had. Having received permission, she ran out of the bathroom. She was dressed in a red jumpsuit and red sneakers. She seated herself on the second bed opposite Roland. Her feet barely touched the floor.

Roland continued to stare at her, perplexed. She glanced over at him, then pointed up at the television.

"See, you've already got it on."

Roland looked up at the television screen and saw images from *The Wizard of Oz*. The happy sound of munchkins filled the room. He looked back at the girl. Her eyes were glued to the screen. Roland struggled to make sense of her presence. The girl could sense his confusion and addressed it.

"Some of these units are connected. Pretty weird, huh?"

Roland nodded and sat on his bed.

The little girl pointed toward the TV screen. "Look—I love this part."

They were complete strangers, yet she was instantly and totally at ease with him. One would have thought them to be old friends or related. Roland began to feel a bit self-conscious about his staring and tried to look at the television. She could sense his unease and decided to make friends.

"My name's Karla Rivera. Karla with a K."

"Nice to meet you, Karla." The longer he sat in her

presence, the more Roland relaxed. He wished that he had something to offer her.

Karla reached in her pocket and removed two fun size bags of Skittles candy, tossing one over to Roland.

"Catch. These are my favorites."

Karla opened the bag and popped a piece of candy into her mouth. She never stopped looking at the television screen and sometimes sang along with the songs or mimicked the dialogue. Roland placed his candy on the nightstand. He hadn't seen *The Wizard of Oz* in years. Maybe it was time for a revisit. He lay back down on his bed, positioning his pillow so that he could still see both the television and Karla, who was seated at the foot of the other bed with her back to him.

Though she'd seen the film many times, Karla remained enthralled by the colorful spectacle. From time to time, she'd turn around to make sure Roland hadn't missed a good part. Her gap- toothed smile was endearing and her laughter melodious. "I like the flying monkeys."

Roland liked them, too. The last time he'd seen this movie was with his own children. Or was it his grandchildren? It was so long ago. Regardless, it was a sweet memory now rekindled. Roland smiled at the thought.

"I wish I had some ruby red slippers," Karla mused.

"Oh, yeah? Where would you go?" He'd forgotten how entertaining it was to talk with young children.

"To see my grandmother. She lives in Catemaco. That's in Mexico."

"I know. It's a special place."

"My *Lita* is special. Sick people come to her from all over, and she makes them well." Karla turned to address Roland face-to-face. She looked concerned. "You're not sick, are you?"

"No, I'm fine."

Karla was relieved. "Well, that's good. But if you were, *Lita* could fix you. She can fix anyone and make them all better. Do you have children?"

"I've got children and grandchildren, too. But they're not children anymore." Roland laughed.

"Okay."

It was well past midnight. Karla was still wide awake and wired in the land of Oz. Her cheerful demeanor was a calming presence. Roland struggled to keep his eyes open. Perhaps, if he closed them for only a moment or two, it would be enough to revive him for more conversation. It would have been rude to fall asleep.

* * *

When Roland awoke, he was covered with a blanket. There was a window by the entrance door, and the sun shone through the thin curtains. Roland sat upright and wiped his eyes. The television was off. Karla was gone. What time was it, anyway? There was no clock on the wall. Roland looked on the nightstand and remembered he'd left his cellphone in the pocket of his trench coat. He uncovered himself, stood and went to the closet. He removed his cellphone from his coat and discovered the battery was now dead. What's more, he'd left the charger in the car.

Roland slipped on his shoes and exited his room. As he headed across the parking lot, he noticed Leo waving to him from inside the office. Roland waved back. He opened his car and removed the charger. He turned to head back to his room when he saw Leo still waving. Roland entered the office to find Leo behind the counter, pouring himself a cup of coffee.

"Good morning, Mister Griffin—or rather, good afternoon. Just in time for some coffee. Did you sleep okay?"

"Yeah, I did. What time is it, anyway?"

"Almost three."

"Almost three?" Roland was surprised. "Wow. I didn't mean to sleep that late."

"You didn't end up donating to charity after all, did you?" Leo shot Roland a sly wink.

"Oh, no." Roland laughed. "But I did have fun last night. I watched *The Wizard of Oz* with my next-door neighbor."

"Your next-door neighbor?"

"Yeah, a little kid from next door came over and watched TV."

Leo looked confused. "A little kid from next door came over and watched TV?"

Roland noted Leo's confusion, but he didn't understand it. "Uh, yeah, but it was okay. I didn't mind."

"Are you sure?"

"Am I sure? Of course I'm sure. Why wouldn't I be?

Leo came from behind the counter. He opened the office door and ushered Roland outside, leading him over to the apartment units. As they walked, he said nothing, but he was clearly perplexed. Leo passed the door to Roland's unit, unit number one, and continued on to unit number two, unlocking the door. Before he opened it, he looked over at Roland.

"Somebody came from next door, you said?"

Leo opened the door and pushed it open completely, revealing a storage room. The room was jampacked with stacked pieces of furniture, shelves bulging with boxes, industrial cleaning machines, and rolls of carpeting propped up against the wall. Everything in the room was covered with cobwebs.

"Somebody came from over here?"

Roland stepped inside and looked around. He was shocked. "I don't understand."

"Well, that makes two of us. This has been a storage room for as long as I can remember. And I've been here quite a while."

"I don't understand. She came from over here."

"She who?"

"The kid. The little girl. I'll show you." Roland led Leo out of the storage room and back over to his unit. He opened the door and headed to the bathroom. "She came out of here last night. She said they—somebody—wouldn't let her watch her movie. I heard knocking from in here."

"From inside this bathroom?"

"It woke me up. She came out and asked if she could watch my TV. She said some of the units were connected."

Roland approached the wall opposite the bathroom door and examined the door frame with his hand.

"There might have been a door there at one time, maybe back when they first built the joint. But I can assure you, there aren't any connected rooms now."

Roland backed away from the wall, visibly shaken. He walked out of the bathroom and looked at the edge of the bed where Karla had been sitting. He saw a stray piece of candy on the floor and anxiously picked it up.

"Look!" Roland said, remembering. He rushed over to the nightstand and found the bag of candy lying where he'd left it. He was relieved. "Here's the proof. She gave me this candy last night. I don't eat candy. Here's the proof."

Leo stared at Roland, not quite sure what to think.

Roland panicked. "I swear to God, I'm not making this up. And I didn't dream it either. She was here. She was here!"

"Okay, okay. If you say she was—"

Roland wasn't about to be patronized. "She *was* here, I'm telling you!" He held up the bag of Skittles as truth. "I've got the proof right here!"

Roland was overwhelmed by the unexplainable. He'd awoken from a blissful sleep and stepped into a nightmare. He sat down on the bed, clutching the bag of Skittles in desperation. It seemed the only proof of his sanity. Leo sat down beside him.

"I believe you."

Roland looked at Leo for confirmation. "You do? Really?"

"If you say it happened, it happened."

"You don't think I'm crazy? Or that I dreamed it?"

"Nope. I believe you. We just need to figure out what it means, that's all. Come on."

The two men exited Roland's unit and returned to the office. Roland seated himself on one of the barstools, as Leo returned to his spot behind the counter, pouring Roland a cup of coffee.

"Okay. Now run it by me again. And go slow."

"I heard knocking coming from inside the bathroom. She came in and asked if she could watch my TV. We watched *The Wizard of Oz* together until I fell asleep. We talked. She was a sweet little girl. Friendly. About seven or eight years old. Dressed in red. She told me her name. Her name is Karla… Karla with a K."

"Karla? Did she have a last name?"

"Rivera. Karla Rivera."

Leo thought for a moment. He reached down and brought a laptop computer from the lower part of the counter and placed it on top. Roland stared down at his coffee cup as if into an abyss.

"You really believe me? Right?" Roland's plea was almost pitiful. He could imagine how insane he must have sounded.

"If you said you watched *The Wizard of Oz* with a little girl last night, then that's what you did."

"So, what's going on?"

Leo didn't answer. He was too focused on his computer. When he finally looked up, he seemed uneasy. "Karla with a K Rivera?"

"Yes, that's her name."

Leo turned the computer around, positioning the screen to where Roland could now see it. There was an image of a newspaper, the cover of the *Las Vegas Review-Journal.* The headline read "Missing Child Feared Abducted." Below the headline was a smiling, gap-toothed photo of Karla dressed in red. Roland put down his coffee cup and stood up from the bar stool, frozen.

Leo studied the screen a bit closer. "That's interesting. Take a look at that date. That's nine years ago."

Roland felt as though he'd been struck in the head by a hammer, only to have his head now explode into pieces. He backed away from the counter, teetering from side-to-side, as if his knees were about to buckle. He became nauseated.

Leo rushed from around the counter, seating him on the couch in the corner. There was a small trash can beside the couch. Leo managed to hand it to Roland in time to catch the projectile vomiting. When Roland finished, Leo sat beside him. Roland broke down and wept uncontrollably. He tried to speak, but only gibberish came out. Leo comforted him.

"Just take it easy. Take it easy. We'll figure this out."

Roland clutched at Leo's arm, and the look in his eyes was near hysterical. He was still unable to form coherent sentences.

Leo was supportive. "I know it's crazy, but it happened. We've just got to figure out what it means." Leo returned to his place behind the counter and finished reading the newspaper article. Roland sat with his head in his hands. He was drained of tears.

"Poor little thing. She went out to buy some candy and never made it back home."

Roland finally managed to speak, but it was more of a whisper. "It's impossible."

"Well, it happened, so it's not impossible. Besides, this is Las Vegas, so anything is possible. By the way, *The Wizard of Oz* wasn't on last night. You might as well know that, too."

Roland pulled the bag of Skittles from his pocket, clutching it with both hands.

Leo placed the computer back behind the counter and printed out a copy of the newspaper article detailing Karla's disappearance. He came from around the counter and seated himself beside Roland. He looked at Karla's picture.

"You mentioned you'd served overseas. So, you've seen war. Well, there's another kind of war going on out here, too; a war nobody ever talks about. It's the war on children. I think Karla Rivera is one of the casualties."

"What do you mean?"

"I mean just what I said. There's a war on children. It's a secret; maybe the biggest secret in the whole world. And it's been going on since ancient times. Look at world history. Look closely. There's a dark thread weaving its way through the ages. That thread is the murder of children. A literal war on children. Child sacrifice takes many forms. The spirit of Molech is alive and well."

Roland sat back and listened.

"Our leaders never discuss it. Liberal or conservative, makes no difference. Neither group says a word. But they know all about it. They're too informed not to know. But they're compromised, so they say nothing. Then there's the churches. Church pews all over the world are filled with a ready-made army of soldiers who could be fighting this war.

But they're confused, so they do nothing. When it comes to the war on children, the church is as useless as the state."

Roland sat up. He took the newspaper article from Leo and looked at the picture of Karla.

"Obviously, the media never talks about it. Why would it? The media isn't designed to enlighten people. The media is in the blackout business. The media is designed to keep people in the dark, and that's exactly what it does. So, there's a complete media blackout when it comes to this issue. The last place you'll hear about the war on children is on the six o'clock news. The media makes sure this secret stays a secret."

"But why?"

"Why has there been a war on children for thousands of years? The reason is part of the secret. The most evil thing you can do in this world is to harm a child. In certain circles, doing evil is believed to be empowering, so harming children bestows the greatest power. It actually makes perfect sense in a demonic sort of way. Innocent blood would have to be the most potent and the most powerful. Like I said, the spirit of Molech is alive and well."

"She was so sweet."

"Something happened in that room nine years ago. And there's been no resolution. Last night, Karla reached out to you."

Roland's eyes became fearful again. He'd had a genuine supernatural encounter. Karla's smiling picture now looked frightening, like something from a nightmare. It was the picture of a ghost.

Leo reassured him. "Don't you be afraid of that child. If she didn't like you, she'd have never reached out to you like that in the first place. What Karla needs now is a friend. She reached out into this world and chose you."

"For what?"

"Karla was never seen again. There's been no resolution."

"But what can I do? I'm just an old man. I can barely work my cellphone. How could I possibly resolve something like this?"

"I don't know. But Karla knows. She reached out to you for a reason."

Roland remembered how cheerful and full of life Karla had been. The way she shared her candy. The way she looked back at him, making sure he was enjoying the movie as much as she. He remembered how he had awakened, covered. Now, as he thought of her, the sweet memories of her mitigated his fear. Someone was responsible for Karla's disappearance, and that someone had been walking around free for nine years. Tears again welled in Roland's eyes.

"There's a guy around town," said Leo. "A street guy. His name is Bobby Bradshaw, but he's affectionately known as Trigga. He's bad news—as bad as they come. Prostitution and drugs, but mainly prostitution. Been around for years, too. But he seems to be made of Teflon, so he never gets busted for anything. My guess is that he's an informant, working for Metro. They probably turned him years ago, and he's been on their payroll ever since. He'd be an interesting person to talk to. If anybody's got his ear to the gutter in Las Vegas, it's Trigga. It would be interesting to see if he ever heard anything about this."

"Where do I find him?"

* * *

Cold Cutz barbershop sat in a tiny strip mall on the north end of Martin Luther King Boulevard. Along with the barber shop, there was a beauty shop, a wig shop, a head shop, a storefront church, and June Bug's Funky Fried Chicken. Cold Cutz sat at the very end of the mall. A candy-red Escalade stood out from among the other cars in the lot. The license plate read TRIGGA.

Inside, a barber was diligently carving intricate designs into the hair of a young customer. Several other customers lined the wall directly in front of the barber. They were all focused on their cellphones while awaiting their turn at the razor as Hip-hop provided the soundtrack. There was a booth in the back of the shop, the kind of booth you'd find in a restaurant. It seemed out of place in a barbershop.

The man seated in the booth was so big and wide that he almost took up the entire seat. He wore a Phoenix Suns basketball jersey and several thick gold necklaces. Though he dressed like a modern youth, he was old enough to be the father of anyone in the shop. He was engrossed in the laptop computer before him. He sat facing the door. His name was Trigga.

Roland entered the shop and curious eyes immediately turned in his direction. He was clearly in the wrong place. What would bring an old white man to a barbershop deep in the hood? He surely hadn't come for a fade. Roland paused at the door momentarily, exchanging glances with the perplexed barber and customers. He saw Trigga in the booth at the back and headed in that direction. Trigga was busy posting ads on Craigslist. He glanced up from his computer and saw Roland looking down at him.

Trigga's face was a battle-scarred road map of violent altercations. There was life in his eyes but no trace of humanity. He looked capable of committing any criminal act, with crimes of cruelty a likely favorite. He was a man best avoided at all costs. He looked at Roland, annoyed by his presence, but curious.

"What's up, grandpa? You in the right place? The nursing home is up the street."

Roland removed the newspaper article from his coat, unfolded it, and placed it beside Trigga's laptop.

"I heard you know a lot. I just want to know if you ever heard anything about this little girl."

Trigga looked down at the paper. Roland noted a brief flash of recognition, but Trigga seemed quick to disguise it. He looked up at Roland, making sure to telegraph his disdain.

"What makes you think I know anything about her? What do I look like? Radar?"

Trigga swept the paper away and out of his sight. Dismissed, the paper fell to the floor. Trigga and Roland locked eyes. Trigga looked hostile and confrontational, as he always did. Who did this old white man think he was, anyway? Coming in and asking questions so far from home.

He was lucky he'd caught Trigga in a jovial mood.

Roland reached down and picked up the paper and, as he did, the sleeve of his trench coat rose up his arm. There was a small tattoo on his right forearm. It was a tattoo of three knives embedded in a smiling skull. On either side of the skull were flaming wings.

As Roland stood upright, Trigga noticed the tattoo and was immediately jolted by the sight of it. His rude demeanor changed. His thuggish bravado vanished. He looked at Roland with different eyes now. There was no contempt, but rather fear. And admiration? Trigga suddenly stood and motioned for Roland to join him.

"Sir, I apologize. I overreacted."

Roland seated himself across from Trigga. The other people in the shop had been watching the proceedings all along. They saw the distinct change in Trigga's personality and were amazed. They knew Trigga well. Trigga would rather give head than respect. What had just taken place in the shop was extraordinary. Who was this old dude, anyway?

Trigga avoided eye contact now, as if embarrassed. He seemed ashamed of himself. He found it near impossible to look into the perceptive eyes of a righteous man. Trigga took the paper out of Roland's hand and looked at it again.

"I'm no angel. You can see that. But I would never, ever be involved in something like this." Trigga looked up at Roland, making sure to stress the word *ever*. "I swear to God."

Roland nodded. "Okay."

Trigga looked at the article again. "You gotta draw a line somewhere. Kids are my line." Trigga made quick eye contact, as if to reassure Roland of the sincerity of his words. He needed to be believed. "I've got a code, too." He looked back to the article.

Roland watched Trigga closely. As Trigga stared at Karla's picture, Roland spotted a faint glimmer of humanity in his eyes. "These poor kids. They get snatched, and it ain't always random, either."

"What do you mean?"

"There's something going on out here. And it's deep—deeper than anyone realizes. And it's everywhere, not just here. Kids get snatched. The ones who live get auctioned off, passed around, and dumped. There's an organized agenda behind a lot of this madness. It's the big secret."

"So I hear."

"Certain places in this world know how to cater to people with young tastes. And Las Vegas is one of them. You can get anything you want here. And with the price of life going down like it does, it's not that expensive, either. Vegas is a playground, all right. Especially for a lot of these international super freaks who blow through here. Like the Sharabi brothers. This is their style. They love 'em young and ethnic just like this. Not that I'm saying they had anything to do with her. I don't know. But I know this much. They've had something to do with other little girls just like her. I deal with them because I have to. They like older girls and sometimes boys, too. They do it all. A pulse is their only requirement, and they might not even need that, as freaky as they are. Funny we're even talking about them. They're in town for the weekend."

"They're in town?"

"Yeah. They flew in yesterday, just for the UFC event last night. Tonight, they're hosting a private party. It's being held at the Liberace Plaza, of all places. There's a nightclub at the north end, facing Tropicana. The club is closed for business, been closed for years, but private stuff still goes on there. The Sharabi brothers aren't in town very often, maybe a half dozen times a year, but they're here tonight. I ought to know. I'm supposed to be providing some of the entertainment."

Roland took the article, folded it, and placed it back in his trench coat. He stood, and Trigga was quick to stand, as well. It was time to say goodbye, and Trigga knew he'd have to look Roland in the eyes. Trigga stood with perfect posture, almost at attention, as if to appear as unthug-like as possible. He did everything but salute.

"Thank you for your service." Trigga was sincere.

The two men shook hands. Roland turned and walked away, Trigga's eyes following. His admiration was genuine. The other people in the shop watched Roland leave, then they looked back at Trigga. They knew they'd just witnessed an unbelievable encounter. Who was that old dude, anyway?

* * *

Roland drove along Maryland Parkway, aware of the setting sun. There wasn't much time left in the day, and there was still a lot to do. On the seat beside him was a bouquet of flowers, all red.

As he drove, he found himself more aware of children.

They seemed to be everywhere today. The streets and parks were full of them. They were all so happy and carefree. The sight saddened him. Yesterday, Roland had barely glanced at them or given them a second thought. Today was different. Today, Roland understood the truth. It was getting late. So many of the children seemed too young to be out and unattended. Where were their parents? Is that man following that little girl? Does that little boy know the man he's talking to? Today, the world seemed a far different place. Today, Roland knew the secret. There's a war on children.

Roland pulled to the curb and killed the engine. He saw the tree and recognized it immediately. It sat at the entrance to the park. He knew it was the right tree. Directly across the street was a little grocery store. According to the newspaper article, that's where Karla was last seen when she bought candy for the last time—most likely Skittles, her favorite. Her bike had been found beside the tree at the entrance to the park. Roland was in the right place.

Roland took the bouquet of flowers and stepped from the car. As he headed for the tree, he felt as if he were in a cemetery rather than a neighborhood park. There was activity on the tennis and basketball courts in the distance, but the park entrance was deserted. The tree was tall and thick with two unusually large branches stretching outward, as if welcoming visitors to the park. The shape of the tree suggested life, but the tree itself was dead.

There was a small opening in the tree, large enough for Roland to insert the long stems of the bouquet. It fit perfectly and brought some semblance of life to the dead tree. Roland stood and stared. He thought about Karla's last day in this park. Had she stood in this spot? Perhaps. Who had approached her that day? Had they stood on this spot, as well? Probably. Roland felt his emotions reeling again. He had paid his tribute. It was time to leave. He noticed some litter near the tree, and tossed it in a nearby receptacle. When he turned to go back to his car, he saw them standing, staring at him.

It was a group of five people. There was a woman in the middle, flanked by two people on either side of her. She wore red, the others wore black. They stood hand-in-hand. They watched Roland closely. It was clear that they, too, had come to pay their respects. Roland felt embarrassed by the sight of them and of his presence. He was just a stranger. These people surely belonged here, while he did not. Roland felt like an intruder and quickened his steps as he headed for his car. As he passed the group, he made sure to avoid their eyes.

"Senor, wait." Roland stopped. He was afraid to turn, but he did so. The woman in red stepped away from the group and approached him. Raising the veil that had concealed her face, he noticed a gap in her teeth as she looked at him with a hint of recognition. But how could she know him? Roland had never met this woman.

The woman removed a piece of jewelry from her neck, a small pendant hanging from a leather cord. She moved close enough to place it around Roland's neck. She looked into his eyes. Strange. She now seemed familiar to him. But how? Without a word, she returned to the group. They rejoined hands and walked closer to the tree.

Roland watched them, but only briefly. He hurried back to his car. It would be dark soon. There was work to do.

* * *

Roland sat on his bed, in the exact spot as the night before. He wasn't even sure how long he'd been sitting there. The television was off, and the room was near dark. As he sat, he stared at the bathroom door. The door was closed. He'd made sure to close it. He had hoped to hear the soft knocking again. Karla had reached out to him once. Would she do it again? He hoped. And waited. But she didn't return. Roland was forced to accept that her appearance was meant to be a one-time encounter, never to be repeated. She'd come to him once. Once was enough. Enough to raise his awareness and spark him to action.

It was time to go to work. Roland stood, put on his fedora and trench coat, and looked around the room one last time. He stared at the spot at the foot of the bed where Karla had sat. He grabbed his suitcase from the dresser and exited the room.

It was night. Roland walked over to the office and entered. Leo was seated behind the counter, dressed in a different suit but the same red tie. He was saddened by the sight of Roland. He knew it was time to say goodbye. Leo stood.

"Heading back home now?"

Roland came over to the counter and set down his suitcase. He didn't seat himself at the counter. He didn't answer Leo's question, either. He reached for his wallet.

"What do I owe you?"

Leo was surprised. "Owe me? Why, Mr. Griffin, you don't owe me anything. Your room has been taken care of."

Roland locked eyes with Leo. His first impulse was to refuse the gesture. But it would have been useless to do so, and Roland knew it. Instead, he extended his hand.

"I appreciate everything."

Leo shook Roland's hand. "It was my pleasure, Mr. Griffin, my pleasure indeed. You take good care of yourself now."

To say 'thank you' seemed hardly enough. Roland wanted to say something else, but he wasn't quite sure what. The encounter with Karla had been a terrifying experience that shook him to his core. No one would ever believe it. Yet, Leo did, and not only did he believe it, he understood what the encounter meant. He picked up the pieces of Roland's blown mind and reassembled them. Leo explained the truth and the secret. Karla had reached out to Roland for a reason. Now, he understood why. Roland had been recruited.

Roland picked up his suitcase and left the office.

* * *

Workers dressed in white were scattered throughout the kitchen. The room was awash with manic activity as cooks, servers, waiters, and waitresses worked to provide food and refreshments to the guests partying in the bar and disco. The scene bordered on chaos, and no one seemed to be in charge. At least the music was good. Salsa played from an unseen stereo.

There was a knock at the service entrance door. A couple of workers standing nearby looked at each other, confused. One of them opened the door, and Roland entered. Wheeling a cart stacked with serving pans, he pushed his way past the worker. He was dressed in kitchen worker attire, complete with a long butcher's apron and hat. Because his clothes were red, he stood out from the workers dressed in white. He glanced around the kitchen with a frown.

"Somebody has got some serious explaining to do. Who the hell is in charge around here?"

Roland's presence was forceful and authoritative. The workers looked at one another, bewildered. How were they supposed to know? Roland figured that the kitchen crew had been provided by some local party planner business or temporary agency. He expected a weak chain of command. A young man entered the kitchen from a swinging door that led out to the bar. He carried a tray of dirty glasses he'd brought over from the bar. Unlike the others in the kitchen, he was dressed like a waiter. Several workers immediately pointed at him, and he reacted like a man accused. He'd barely sat the tray down at the dishwashing station before Roland tore into him.

"Are you the one in charge around here? I need some answers—quick."

"Well, Mr. Montoya is actually in charge. He's not here right now. I'm just the—"

"I've been calling here for over two hours, and all I've gotten is an answering machine. Somebody ordered more food for this party." Roland removed detailed documentation from his pocket. He handed the papers to the waiter, who never examined them. "There's more stuff in my car that needs to get in here right away." Roland pointed at two workers. "Go out to my car and bring the rest of that stuff in here now. The doors are unlocked. Get moving."

The two workers complied without question. They opened the service entrance door and hurried out to Roland's car, which was parked nearby. Roland pointed at two other workers, then motioned down at the cart he commandeered.

"I've got salmon and shrimp here. I need for you two to get this stuff on ice. Move it."

The workers did as ordered with spring in their steps. Now, all eyes in the kitchen were focused on Roland. He was clearly the one in charge. He took out his cellphone and pretended to make a call.

"Yeah, it's me. I'm here, finally. This place is a madhouse. But I promise you, before this night is over, I'm gonna find out who dropped the ball. There's no excuse for this level of incompetence. I'll call you back. I've got to keep things moving here. Goodbye."

Roland pretended to end the call, and when he did so, he glanced around the kitchen with judgmental eyes. His presence was transformative. Now the workers moved about the kitchen with urgent efficiency. With the kitchen under control, Roland was able to continue. A waitress entered the kitchen and looked surprised by his presence. Roland walked past her and headed out to view the rest of the establishment.

Roland stepped out of the kitchen and into the music. The volume was near deafening. The area just outside the kitchen appeared to be a foyer, dividing the nightclub into two sections. To Roland's right was a small disco packed with party people. Bistro tables surrounded a dancefloor. To Roland's left was the bar area. Roland walked in that direction, figuring the entrance door would be in that area. The bar itself was ultra-modern, enclosed, and asymmetrical. Three female bartenders kept the drinks flowing for the guests lining the bar. In a lounge area nearby, people kicked back on comfortable furniture. Most eyes were focused on the small stage in the corner where scantily clad young women flashed their wares.

Roland walked deeper into the bar area and scanned the room in search of the entrance. As he pondered its location, two guests entered from a door in the corner, tucked away and out of view. It was easy to miss. Having verified the entrance, Roland now focused on the guests. He positioned himself in the shadows beside a vending machine. There were about a hundred people, mostly male. The females in attendance looked to be elite escorts and international arm candy. There was some muscle in attendance as well. Bigger and badder looking than the other guests, they wore tight, ill-fitting suits and appeared to be 'on the clock." Roland eyed them closely, well aware he'd be dealing with them very shortly. They were most likely highly trained professional fighters and probably armed.

Roland moved away from the vending machine and headed for the disco. He stood out of view and appeared to be supervising the work of the waiters and waitresses. Like the bar area, there looked to be about a hundred guests, mostly female, with many of them on the dance floor. Across the room, three bistro tables had been brought together. Two men sat at the middle table flanked by women on either side. Roland watched them closely.

The Sharabi brothers were middle-aged, Middle Eastern, and looked enough alike to be twins. They even dressed alike, favoring white pinstripe suits modeled after their old school gangster movie heroes. Their facial features were marked by ice-cold eyes and degenerate smiles. Their frequent laughter was loud and perverted. Even from across the club, Roland could feel their evil. Standing nearby on either side of the joined tables was more muscle—two guys as big and bad as anything over at the bar.

Roland had seen enough. He was ready to go to work. He returned to the kitchen, and when he entered, all the workers snapped to attention at the sight of him. A long chrome counter was covered with the many pans of food items he'd brought. A cake box was on the counter, as well. Roland smiled.

"Nice. Now this is what I like to see."

A Puerto Rican waitress entered the kitchen and, to the shock of all the workers, Roland grabbed her and salsa danced, busting moves unexpected from an older white man. The waitress was accomplished as well, and the two danced around the kitchen like seasoned professionals.

When the song finally ended, Roland dipped his partner dramatically, then planted a kiss on her cheek. The workers broke into applause. Roland had transformed the kitchen yet again. Now the atmosphere was borderline festive. The workers pursued their duties with smiling enthusiasm.

Roland went over to the chrome counter and opened the cake box. He removed a disturbing sheet cake. An image of a little girl in pigtails had been expertly drawn on the icing. Beneath the image were the words, *Eat Me, Daddy.* Roland placed the cake on the cart he'd arrived with, along with several saucers. He looked around the kitchen.

"I need something to cut with," Roland ordered to no one worker in particular.

A worker responded and rushed over to him, bringing a medium-sized knife designed for serving cake. Roland frowned. He scanned the kitchen and noticed several knives designed for meat carving hanging on the wall. Pointing to the largest one—a fearsome blade more sword than cake knife—he ordered, "Give me that one."

The worker complied and Roland placed the blade beside the cake with a smile.

"Let's get this party started," Roland added conclusively.

One of the workers held the swinging kitchen door open. Roland pushed the cart out of the kitchen and headed over to the disco. The packed room was still throbbing with excitement. Roland wheeled the cart onto the dance floor, directly into the throng of dancers, and they parted like the Red Sea. He made his way over to where the Sharabi brothers and their guests were seated. Roland positioned the cart directly in front of the brothers' table, and when they saw the cake, they reacted as Roland had expected. They laughed wickedly and applauded.

Roland nodded and smiled. Having presented the cake for viewing, he picked up the knife and plunged it into the groin of each man, then into their bellies. The Sharabi brothers shrieked in mutual agony as blood spurted out of their torn flesh. Roland brought the knife down into the cake, and into the table where it stuck. He thrust both of his hands into the gaping wounds of each brother and pulled out their intestines. With outstretched arms, he held out the long dangling flesh for the mutilated brothers to see. The entire attack was over in a matter of seconds.

The many witnesses to this savagery ran for their lives. Chaos erupted to a Techno soundtrack. The women who had been sitting at the table with the brothers were the first to flee, leaving their high heels behind. The other guests joined them, moving as one, like a stampeding herd. They all stormed out of the disco as if the room were ablaze. The Sharabi brothers both lay on the floor, screaming and convulsing in a sea of blood.

The bodyguards remained. The two men looked formidable and were surely no strangers to extreme violence. But from the startled looks on their faces, they'd never witnessed brutality like this. Roland took advantage of their brief moment of frozen indecision. He pulled the knife out of the table, out of the cake, and attacked. He slit the throat of the man closest to him. The other man reached inside his jacket for a concealed handgun, but Roland spotted him in time enough to send the knife spinning into the man's chest. He dropped to the floor, dead like his associate. Roland ran over to him and pulled the knife out of his body.

Assorted muscle, four in total, charged into the disco from the bar area. They were shocked by the sight of their dead comrades and their butchered employers, still alive and writhing on the floor. Roland advanced toward them, moving out onto the dancefloor. The men surrounded him. Roland attacked. He dived to the floor and severed the Achilles tendon of one badass. When the howling man fell, Roland slit his throat, then rolled back to his feet in time to meet the next badass. The new attacker launched a flying spin kick at Roland's head that could have ended his life. Roland ducked the kick, then lunged forward, stabbing the man repeatedly in the thigh. When the man collapsed, Roland slit his throat.

The remaining two men produced blades of their own and rushed Roland simultaneously. They were skilled knife fighters, and blades sparked against blades as the battle continued. One of the men kicked the knife from Roland's hand, putting him on the defensive. Roland dodged and deflected their stabs and strikes, but not without injury, as he sustained cuts to his hands and face. Roland kicked one attacker in the knee and, as the man fell, Roland snatched him by the head with both hands and twisted his neck to the audible breaking point. He reached inside the man's jacket for the gun he knew would be there. It was a Glock. He pulled it from its holster and fired at the remaining badass. Two shots to the chest, one to the head. Roland tossed the gun aside and headed for the kitchen. He didn't run.

There was bedlam in the bar area as frightened guests scrambled for the entrance door, turning it into a bottleneck.

Roland calmly entered the kitchen and found it empty, the workers no doubt having fled with the rest of the herd. Salsa music was still playing. Roland removed his bloody apron and tossed it along with his hat into a trash can. He opened the service door, exited the kitchen and walked to his car.

As he climbed inside and started the engine, he had the urge for a cigarette, even though he hadn't smoked in years. He drove along the rear wall of the building complex, passing the rear entrances of the various other establishments in the plaza.

Roland finally came to the end of the long structure. He drove the car from behind the building and onto the main parking lot of the plaza. He parked, keeping the motor running. Several yards away he could see the entrance to the nightclub. Roland watched as the terrified guests ran out to their cars to escape the carnage inside.

The sound of sirens signaled the arrival of the police and, moments later, a squad car pulled into the lot. Inside were officers Flanagan and Valdez, with Flanagan at the wheel. He drove close to the entrance of the club and parked. Guests continued pouring out of the club, rushing past the cops as if they didn't see them.

Roland drove over to the squad car and parked beside it just as the officers were climbing out. Officer Flanagan made his way past the guests still hovered around the entrance and entered the club. Officer Valdez was about to follow him, but waited upon seeing Roland arrive. Roland exited his car to confront Officer Valdez.

"That's my mess in there."

To the astonishment of Officer Valdez, Roland opened the rear door of the squad car and climbed inside, closing the door behind him. Officer Valdez stared at Roland, puzzled.

Officer Flanagan returned, standing in the doorway of the club. "It looks like a butcher's shop in there." Officer Flanagan went back inside.

Officer Valdez tapped on the window of the squad car.

Roland lowered the window. "Yes, officer?" Roland's tone was nonchalant.

"What's going on in there?"

"I'm the butcher he's talking about. I told you it was a mess."

Officer Valdez noted the bloodstains on Roland's clothes and the wounds to his face and hands. Clearly, he'd been involved in some extreme violence. Yet his demeanor was oddly relaxed. Valdez climbed back in the passenger seat, activated the radio communicator and called for both an ambulance and additional police backup. He looked at Roland's reflection in the rearview mirror. Roland stared back at him. Who was this old man? Valdez got out of the car and walked over to the club. There were still a few straggling guests, but the parking lot had all but emptied.

Roland had never been in the back of a squad car. It was the last place he'd ever expected to be. Yet there he was. And at his age, no less. There was a first time for everything. What would happen now? What would the charges be? Murder, first degree. How would he plead? Guilty, of course. How many had he killed? Was it six or seven? Maybe eight? Roland had lost track in all the excitement. Of course, the

Sharabi brothers weren't officially dead yet. Roland took special care with them. Their wounds were indeed fatal, but they would die slowly, in agony. They were suffering even now. Showing the brothers their own intestines was a bit theatrical, but it made the point.

Roland thought of his family. He knew he would never see them again. The thought saddened him, but he wasn't ashamed of his actions. He was proud of what he'd done. And the way he'd done it, too. He still had the moves, even with the salsa. That waitress was a great partner, too. Roland smiled, but only for an instant. A wave of regret swept over him with one sad realization. He knew how the media would portray him. He'd be called another nutjob Nam vet who'd gone berserk for whatever reason and carved up some people. He'd be called a crazy, homicidal old man who never got properly treated for PTSD. That bothered him far more than his family. Nam vets never got the respect they deserved. Roland's butchery would only serve to perpetuate the undeserved stereotypes. It was the first time he felt any guilt.

Officer Valdez came out from the club again and returned to the squad car. He stood beside Roland's window and looked down at the old man. Roland sat back in the seat, deep in thought, staring straight ahead.

"So, that's your mess in there? All of it?"

Roland looked up into his eyes. "Every bit of it. But nobody's dead who ain't supposed to be."

There was something unusual in Roland's eyes and demeanor, something that made Officer Valdez certain he wasn't dealing with an ordinary man. The back seat of a squad car is reserved for criminals. The man seated there now reflected nobility, not criminality. It was obvious. He not only didn't belong there, it was a crime to have him there. Officer Valdez, though not as old as Roland, wasn't a young man, either. He had been on the force and on the Earth long enough to know a truly decent man when he saw one. Besides, this was Las Vegas. A decent anything stood out like a nun in a brothel. A lot of death had been dealt in that nightclub tonight, but this noble man was no murderer. There had to be an explanation.

Roland absentmindedly wiped at some dried blood on his neck, causing the pendant he'd been wearing to fall out of his shirt into view. When Officer Valdez saw the pendant, his eyes went wide with recognition. It was no ordinary piece of jewelry, and the sight of it confirmed his intuition. Only an extraordinary person would be in possession of this particular pendant.

"That jewelry you're wearing there. Where did you get that?"

Roland had forgotten he was even wearing it. He grasped the pendant and caressed it between his fingers as he thought of the park and the tree and the mysterious woman.

"A woman gave it to me. Just today."

Officer Valdez stepped back from the car. He was no closer to understanding what had happened in the nightclub, but he knew that the man in the back of the squad car was innocent of any crimes. He'd swear his life on it.

Officer Flanagan walked out of the nightclub and rejoined his partner at the squad car. He glanced at Roland seated in the back seat. "I guess you can't judge a book by its cover."

"How's your mom doing these days?" Asked Officer Valdez of his partner, awaiting a response. The question was both odd and out of the blue, leaving Officer Flanagan perplexed. Valdez cleared up his confusion. "Your mom got that surgery she needed. And I'm glad she got it, too. She deserved it. Nobody needed to know where the money came from. I looked the other way that night."

Officer Flanagan's face was a sudden mix of shock and shame. Officer Valdez had just unearthed a controversial memory. He offered no response. Approaching sirens could be heard in the distance.

"Tonight, it's your turn. Tonight, you're going to look the other way." Valdez said, gesturing toward Roland. "Because the only place that man is going is free."

Officer Flanagan didn't understand, but he didn't argue, either. He watched as Officer Valdez opened the door for Roland. Roland got out of the squad car and locked eyes with Valdez, who took hold of the pendant and put it back down into Roland's shirt. He felt the need to say something more to the mysterious old man. "Thank you for your service."

Roland nodded. He didn't understand, but he was grateful. He walked over to his car, climbed inside, and drove out of the plaza just as the ambulance and backup police were arriving.

* * *

Roland spent the night in a Walmart parking lot in the front seat of his car. He'd taken a bird bath in the bathroom sink at a convenience store, then changed into clean clothes. He filled up his tank and studied his map over coffee. There were two stops he needed to make before he left Las Vegas for good.

The late morning traffic was light and, as Roland drove, he again focused on the children. They were everywhere. Had the birthrate exponentially increased in recent years? As he cruised by the familiar park, many of them were playing there today. Smiling, happy, and carefree. He thought of Karla. The red bouquet remained in the tree.

Roland turned off of Eastern Avenue and onto Fremont Street. He felt compelled to pass the motel once more. There was time. He drove for a few blocks, then pulled over and parked. He wasn't lost. He knew exactly where he was. He'd only been there the night before. But something was different. More than different, something was gone. Roland climbed out of his car and stood across the street from the motel, from where the motel had been standing only yesterday. Today, the motel grounds were occupied by busy workers and heavy equipment. The motel had been torn down completely.

* * *

Jill secured all the detailed notecards for Reuben's latest tale in a rubber band and stared at them. She had asked for a ghost story. Reuben had delivered that and more. What began as a creepy ghost story evolved into a tale of a holy quest with an unlikely warrior.

Reuben's magic was certainly consistent. Once again, he'd proven himself to be a major storytelling talent. It was becoming near impossible to walk the tightrope of deception. Fortunately, Jill remembered that Reuben wasn't particularly enthusiastic about this story anyway. She'd keep that in mind as she presented her latest lying critique.

"You did it again, Reuben. Another great one. You caught me by surprise with that one, too. You went from the *Twilight Zone* to… I don't know… the Terminator zone with that ending. I loved it. It had a tight little plot, great pacing, cool characters. You know how to bring dimension to your characters, that's for sure. That story has everything going for it. But there's a problem, and it's a big one."

"What's that?"

"The modern audience just isn't ready for Grandpa Rambo. Don't get me wrong, he's a great character, and I love him to death, but he'd never fly. Not these days. You know as well as I do that the horror market is youth driven. It's always been that way, and I don't see it changing in the near future."

"Yeah, you're right about that. Plus, the story isn't even all that scary either. I told you it wasn't."

Jill was relieved her critique hadn't offended Reuben or put him on the defensive. Feeling agile in her deception, she took the opportunity to dip into Reuben's magic well yet again. It seemed inexhaustible.

"You know, with your whole concept set here in Sin City, don't you have something with more of a Vegas vibe—that vibe you were talking about earlier? Don't you have a story that gets to the heart of what Las Vegas is really about? Like a story about gambling or—"

Reuben burst into laughter. "Are you serious? What do you want, a haunted casino? The slot machine from hell?" Reuben's tone was cynical. "Gambling? So, you think Vegas is all about gambling, huh? You and everybody else. I've got news for all of you. Las Vegas is a yin yang symbol, but people only see the one aspect and never the other. I'm here to tell you, Las Vegas is as much about sex as gambling, maybe more."

Jill was elated by Reuben's enthusiastic response. She'd struck a nerve. Her intuition told her Reuben was about to give her the Big O.

"Well, tell me a Vegas sex story. You've got me all wired. You've taken me to the edge four times in a row. You need to give me all you've got with this one, Reuben. You know what I'm saying? You've got me so close. I need to get off this time."

"You and everybody else. That's why the world really comes to Las Vegas—to get off. If New York is the Big Apple, and New Orleans is the Big Easy, then Las Vegas is the Big O. People come here for a feeling they can't get in Milwaukee—or Macau, for that matter. It's like I told you before, the Vegas Vibe is a maximizer. So, food tastes better, drinks hit harder, dope gets you higher, and you come like a freight train."

Jill smiled in anticipation of the pleasure awaiting her with the next story. She readied a new stack of note cards to fill with Reuben's magical ideas.

"There's an old saying here—once you find Las Vegas, Las Vegas finds you. Well, here's a story that explains what that means."

Babylon Wood

Night. A taxicab cruised northbound on Las Vegas Boulevard with three, twenty- something young men crammed into the backseat. Maxwell sat in the middle. Curtis and Norby, sitting on either side, were mesmerized by the frenzied sights and sounds of the Strip through their open windows. As they ogled the famous neon landmarks, they looked like two kids at Disneyland.

Maxwell stared straight ahead. He shared neither their enthusiasm nor interest. He was in a sour mood. He wanted to be somewhere else. The driver looked like a retired Elvis impersonator, complete with jet black pompadour and shades.

"So where are you guys from, anyway?"

"Milwaukee," answered Curtis.

"Milwaukee? Jeffrey Dahmer, right? How do you like Las Vegas?"

Curtis and Norby responded simultaneously with glee. "Love it!"

Maxwell offered his own opinion. "Loathe it."

The driver was surprised. "Loathing Las Vegas? Don't

hear that too often. What's the problem?"

"It's simple. Your famous city is overrated, and *wildly* overrated at that. I'm starting to think we got here too late. Like thirty years too late."

Curtis and Norby shot annoyed glances at Maxwell, who always seemed to travel with his own personal storm cloud. When he was in a particularly bad mood like tonight, he didn't just rain on parades, he pissed on them.

"Here we go," sighed Norby with an eyeroll. "I can hardly wait."

"What's your problem now?"

"Vegas might have been the shit back in the day, but that was then. It's a different town now."

The driver agreed with Maxwell. "You're absolutely right. It was a different town when the mob was running it. Anybody will tell you that. The entertainment was better, the food was cheaper, the slots were looser, and the people were friendlier. You'd still leave broke, but you always felt like a winner. It's not like that anymore."

"I bet the chicks were hotter, too," said Maxwell.

"Yeah, well, the advantage with chicks back in the day was you *knew* they were chicks. It's hard to know now. Before you take a chick home these days, you'd better scrutinize 'em forensic style, just to be on the safe side. Trans this, trans that, preop, postop. I've seen some of everything in that back seat. Women have always been complicated, but now it's ridiculous."

Maxwell lit a cigarette, as he continued his negative appraisal. "Whatever it is that happens in Vegas can stay in

Vegas as far as I'm concerned. For all the so-called sin I've seen so far, I feel like I'm in Mayberry. This place is a joke. I knew coming here was a dumb idea."

"What about last night?" Asked Norby.

"What about last night? We went to a strip club. Big deal. They've got strip clubs in Milwaukee. If anybody knows that, you guys do."

"Not totally nude, they don't," Curtis replied, smiling at the memory.

Maxwell frowned. "Totally nude," he spat out. "Let me tell you something. When I order a beer, and the waitress says twenty dollars, I'm totally crazy if I don't slap that bitch and walk out the door. Strippers are *your* bag, not mine. That's why you guys think this joint is so special." Maxwell shook his head. "Strippers," he repeated in disgust.

The driver chimed in. "Strippers. Yeah, there's a lot of 'em here, all right, that's for sure. There's probably more strippers in Nevada than people in Texas. Nevada doesn't even need a state flag. All it needs is the pole."

"I just don't get the appeal of strippers. I never did. What's the point? What's the point of paying money to *not* get satisfied? What sense does that make? It's crazy, not to mention expensive. And totally nude? So what? Did you actually *get* any of that totally *nudeness*? No. Hell, no. The only thing you got was broke. Hard up and broke. Or broke, then hard up. Whatever. And you came all the way to Las Vegas to do it."

"But were they real chicks? That's the question," the driver laughed.

Curtis didn't care for the question. "You'd better believe they were real chicks. I damn sure wouldn't have been there if they hadn't been."

Maxwell was tickled by Curtis's knee jerk reaction. "Yeah? You sure? You've had what… one girlfriend in your whole life, right? I hate to break it to you, player, but one girl doesn't exactly make you an expert on female reality. Technically, you're only one girl away from virginity." Maxwell laughed. "Some expert you are. You're a yellow belt, and you just got it, too."

The driver continued. "The only reason I ask is that they've got transexual strip clubs here, too. You wouldn't be the first guys who accidentally—"

"Those chicks were real." Curtis was indignant.

Norby agreed, indignantly. "I was there, too. They were real, all right."

Maxwell took a drag off his cigarette. "And what do you know about a real chick? You've had what… two chicks in your whole life? That makes you twice as experienced as the expert over here. Yellow belts. Both of you."

"It doesn't take a black belt to know what a real chick is." Norby was sick of Maxwell's attitude. "I ain't never been fooled."

"Me, neither," added Curtis.

The driver was amused by the overt homophobic defensiveness. "Well, the tranny strippers they got out here are in a whole different league. They look just like chicks. Some of 'em even look *better* than chicks. Seriously. They've got the makeup down. And they know how to tuck their junk for the gig. Lots of guys have been fooled. Believe me, I've heard plenty of stories. Just the other day, I heard about this—"

Curtis angrily interrupted. "Hey, man, just cause I'm from Milwaukee doesn't mean I'm an idiot, okay? I know the difference between a dude and a chick."

"Same here," added Norby.

Like the driver, Maxwell found their homophobia entertaining. It was more fun than anything else he'd experienced in Vegas thus far. He decided to play along with the driver.

"I don't believe it. Three straight guys come cross country from square-ass Milwaukee to Sin City and end up in a tranny strip club. Ain't that a bitch? That's what I get for running with rookie yellow belts. Good thing you didn't bring any chicks back to the hotel. We'd have gotten gang-banged."

Curtis could barely control his anger. He'd had enough of Maxwell. "The only thing that makes you happy is making other people miserable. That's your idea of fun."

Norby agreed. "Only you could have a bad time in Las Vegas. You can't have a good time anywhere. Ever since we got here, the only person not having fun is you. We've been having a blast. Eating, drinking, gambling, strip clubs—"

"Totally nude," added Curtis.

"Totally nude. But nothing—and I mean nothing—is ever right for you."

Maxwell flicked his cigarette out the window. "Strip clubs aren't right for me, that's for sure. They don't get me off, they piss me off. Yeah, I'm in a bad mood, all right. You'd better believe it. I thought I was coming to Sin City, not Salt Lake City. This is no city of sin, not from what I've seen so far. Don't call yourself Babylon if you can't represent, that's all I'm saying."

Maxwell pointed out the window at the gaudy monuments and the horde of tourists. The sight disgusted him. "The only thing Las Vegas represents is the decline and fall of western civilization. Look at this shit. But you know something? I could even deal with that if it lived up to all the hype. But it doesn't, and that's what pisses me off about this place. Sin City my ass. Las Vegas is no Babylon. Las Vegas is just like a strip club. Something stupid designed to separate a fool from his money. A fool and his money are lucky to get together in the first place."

"I don't care what you say, this place rocks," Curtis said. "There's no place like Vegas." Curtis turned away from Maxwell and looked out the window again. He was done with the discussion.

Maxwell wasn't going to let it go. "Do you even know what Babylon is? What it was? What went on there? Compared to Babylon, Las Vegas is Chuck E. Cheese. What do yellow belts know about anything, anyway? Here's what I know—I'm not like you guys. I've had more than two chicks. *Way* more. I'm a man of the world—a real player. And because of that, I've got special needs. Okay? I need something a lot more adrenalized than this meager little nothing they're serving up here. I didn't come all the way from square-ass Milwaukee to world famous Sin City to stay soft. I came to get hard."

"You want the wood. The Babylon Wood," said the driver.

"Babylon Wood? What's that?" asked Maxwell.

"That's the ultimate erection."

"The ultimate erection? Now there's a subject deserving of further exploration. We've been talking about dumb shit all night long. We need to be talking about this. Talk."

"Babylon Wood is, well, rigidity on a whole new level."

"Rigidity?" Maxwell laughed. "I think that's the first time I've ever heard that word used. Sounds nasty, too. And on a whole new level? Damn."

"Yup," the driver said. "The most intense sexual experience possible. Or even imaginable."

"Is it possible?" Maxwell replied. "I can't imagine."

"And the only place in the whole world where you can get that experience is right here. Right here in fabulous Las Vegas."

Maxwell sat up from his seat and broke into applause. He was borderline giddy at the prospect of such pleasure. "You see? You see? I *knew* coming to Las Vegas was a great idea. Let's go. Right now. Forget about some Thai food. I ain't even hungry, anyway."

The driver laughed. "Babylon Wood is just an obscure, old school expression. It's a term for what guys are *really* looking for when they come to Sin City, which is ecstasy in the extreme. But it's just a metaphor. It doesn't really exist. I was just playing with you. Sorry."

Maxwell was shocked. The driver had been quite convincing. "Say what? A metaphor? Are you serious? You've gotta be kidding. You'd *better* be kidding. After a commercial that stimulating, you're going to tell me the product doesn't even exist? I believe you just blew your tip, Mister Cab Driver."

"Oops, sorry about that. I got carried away." The driver laughed. "I've been told I've got a warped sense of humor."

"You don't hear me laughing back here, do you?" Replied Maxwell.

The intersection of Las Vegas Boulevard and Sahara Avenue is one of the brightest and busiest in the city. As the driver waited for the red light to turn, Curtis and Norby were enthralled by the neon spectacle spread out before them. Maxwell sat back, looking straight ahead. His mood had worsened again. The driver turned right with the green and continued, heading east on Sahara.

"So, how'd you guys hear about the Pearl Pagoda?"

"All the reviews said it was world class," answered Norby.

"It is. One of the best."

There were no landmarks or neon spectacle, but the traffic was far less frenzied. The area was a mix of residential and business. While it wasn't the skids, the neighborhood had clearly seen better days. It was a marked difference from the sparkling madness of the Strip only blocks away. Norby noticed the tall, white containment wall on the right that enclosed the Commercial Center. Back in the glory days of Las Vegas, the Commercial Center had been a thriving retail and restaurant destination. But in recent years, the Center had lost much of its luster and popularity due to the changing neighborhood. Bordered by high white walls, from the outside, it resembled a fortress.

The driver turned into the entrance of the Center. Though low on glitz, it had a unique charm. The tall white containment walls hid a sprawling shopping complex lined with businesses along the inner perimeter, many of which were closed. There was also an island of businesses in the middle of the vast parking lot. It was an eclectic mix. There were ethnic restaurants, storefront churches, karaoke bars, fetish clothing stores, and even an Asian supermarket. Along with an assortment of LGBT friendly establishments, there was even a swingers club. Being enclosed, the Center actually felt like a fortress. Though the Center was a shadow of its former self, it still remained a favorite spot for many. Tonight, as on most nights, the parking lot was packed, and people filled the sidewalks. The night air crackled with excitement. Curtis and Norby were fascinated by the new sights and sounds. Even Maxwell's curiosity was piqued. "Now this is different. This is working. I like this."

"There's a lot more to Las Vegas than the Strip," said the driver. "And the Commercial Center is the perfect example. There's some of everything up in here." The driver came to a stop in front of a restaurant where a small crowd gathered out front. "Well, here we are. Your taste buds are in for an experience."

"Yeah, well it's not a taste bud experience I'm looking for," Maxwell uttered sarcastically. "They've got rice in Milwaukee."

The driver laughed. "I'm really sorry I did that to you."

"Think so? Wait'll you see your tip."

Curtis and Norby climbed out of the cab, saying nothing

to the driver. He'd left a bad taste in their mouths as well. They headed over to the restaurant.

"It looks kind of busy," said the driver to Maxwell. "I'm not surprised, though. Unless you've got a reservation, you might have a wait on your hands."

"It doesn't matter. I'm not even hungry."

"What have you guys got going on after dinner?"

"What else? Another strip club."

"Well, FYI, there just happens to be a strip club in here. But I'd better warn you now, it's a tranny joint. I just figured I'd give you the heads up."

Maxwell laughed. "Really? That's great. After dinner, I'll take the rookies but not tell them what's up. I might end up having some fun tonight after all."

"That'll be thirty dollars."

Maxwell pulled two twenties from his pocket and handed them to the driver. "Keep it. Thanks for pulling my coat about the tranny joint. I'll do my best to forget about your metaphor."

"Thanks. Honestly, I really am sorry about that. But you know, the night is young. You might just find what you're looking for after all."

"I doubt it. I've seen enough, anyway. What happens in Vegas must be happening to somebody else cause it sure ain't happening to me."

Maxwell climbed out of the cab. Curtis and Norby were nowhere in sight. The driver poked his head out of the window.

"You're in Las Vegas, my friend. And in Las Vegas, anything is possible."

"Right. Take it easy."

"You, too. Thanks."

As the driver drove off, Curtis and Norby emerged from the Thai restaurant and approached Maxwell. Norby was uptight. "That place is packed. It's gonna be at least an hour before we can get a table in there. What do you want to do?"

Maxwell looked around the enormous retail complex that engulfed them. "I like this joint. Let's just chill, walk around, and check out the situation. It's got a better vibe than the Strip, anyway. I don't mind this."

Maxwell walked away, leaving his friends to play catch-up. As the trio walked, they were fascinated by the diverse businesses they encountered. The people they passed along the way were a colorful mix of out-of-towners, cool locals, and freaks.

Maxwell was amazed. "The coolest place in Vegas ain't even on the Strip. Figures."

Maxwell stopped to light a cigarette. As he exhaled, he heard the sound of organ music and turned around to find a storefront establishment with no signage. The music was coming from inside. Curious, Maxwell tossed the cigarette and walked to the entrance. "I want to check this out."

Curtis and Norby followed Maxwell inside and at first, it was difficult to tell what the place was. Clearly, it was still in transition. Several workers were actively engaged in renovation work. Some were painting walls and laying carpet. Others were positioning long benches and chairs into neat, orderly rows. A small stage had already been built and at the front.

Reverend Gator was seated onstage, surrounded by several keyboards on stands. He was focused on the organ directly in front of him, and he was in total command of the instrument. The music he played was a mix of gospel, blues, funk, and even classical. He had the room rocking, and many of the workers were grooving to the music.

Reverend Gator welcomed the trio of newcomers with a smile and a nod. Maxwell led his friends over to a bench in front of the stage where they seated themselves. Reverend Gator proceeded to dazzle them with his music. He ended his presentation with a lightning-fast run and a soul-stirring final chord. The trio broke into an enthusiastic round of applause.

The reverend stood and took a humble bow. He was a slender, attractive, older black man with an unusually large gray afro. He was casually dressed in jeans and a t-shirt, but he wore a shiny pair of blue alligator Stacy Adams shoes.

"Nice. I finally found something good in this sorry city," Maxwell said sincerely.

Reverend Gator sat down and resumed playing, only now the music was quite different. It sounded like funeral music. "And how are the youngbloods doing this evening?"

Maxwell had taken a liking to the reverend. "Fine now. Man, I'm glad we ran into you. I love the way you play. That was great. What is this place, anyway?"

"Well, in another week, it's going to be the Crossroads Tabernacle."

"Crossroads Tabernacle? This is a church?"

"That's right. And you and your friends are invited to come back."

"Thanks for the invitation, but we're leaving in the morning. I'm Maxwell, and this is Curtis and Norby."

Curtis and Norby waved, and the reverend acknowledged them. He continued playing the somber music, but at a lower volume. "Very nice to meet you. They call me Reverend Gator. Where are you visiting from?"

"Milwaukee," answered Curtis.

"Milwaukee? Jeffrey Dahmer, right?"

"Where are you from?" asked Maxwell. "You don't look like Vegas to me."

"I'm not. I'm born and raised in the greatest city in the whole world—New Orleans. Or N'awlins.

"Figures, with the way you play."

"Are you a player?" The reverend winked as he posed the question, well aware of its double entendre.

"Of females, absolutely," Maxwell answered proudly. "Music? Absolutely not. But I am a patron of the art. I know talent when I hear it, that's for sure. That's some of the best playing I've ever heard. Seriously. I don't mean to be insulting, but what are you doing here? America is no place for you. You need to be in Europe. Musical OGs get mad respect overseas. You've got the talent. You've got the look, too. Europe would be all over you in a heartbeat."

Reverend Gator nodded with a humble smile. "As a matter of fact, I spent a lot of time in Europe. Many years, actually. You're very perceptive."

"Where abouts?"

"I traveled all over playing in bands. I'd bounce back and forth between Europe and the States, but I was mainly overseas.

I've lived in France, Germany, and the Netherlands."

"Figures. I'm not surprised one bit. Europeans know their music, especially black American music. I bet they treated you like royalty, too."

"Yes, they did. Coming back was quite an adjustment."

"So, why'd you come back?"

"Why? Well, Europe loves me, but America needs me, especially a city like Vegas. So, tell me, how did you youngbloods end up here at the Commercial Center?"

"We're having dinner over at the Pearl Pagoda," answered Norby. "We're just waiting on a table."

Reverend Gator nodded. He studied the trio with perceptive eyes. "So, what have the youngbloods been up to in Sin City?"

"Oh, just checking out the tourist attractions. Lots to see," answered Curtis.

"Lots to get into, that's for sure," said the reverend.

"Or so I thought." Maxwell replied.

The reverend picked up on the cynical tone. "What happened? Didn't find what you were looking for?"

Maxwell smiled but didn't answer. Reverend Gator continued his somber music, never taking his eyes off of the trio. "Don't get quiet on me now. We can talk." The reverend was in the mood for conversation.

"Well, this is a church," Maxwell said. "Some things you just don't discuss in a church."

Reverend Gator looked surprised. "Yeah? Like what? You ought to be able to discuss anything in church. That's what church is for. Churches today don't understand that. And that's one reason why people don't go. This church is different. It's sure going to be. Everything is up for discussion at the Crossroads Tabernacle."

The trio began to squirm uncomfortably, and Reverend Gator enjoyed watching them. "You know what I think? I think you youngbloods are looking for more than just blackjack, booze, and buffets. You're looking for something else."

"You got that right. And it ain't Celine Dion, either."

Maxwell's joke made everyone laugh, including Reverend Gator. But the reverend understood. "I know exactly what you're looking for. You're looking for flesh, what else? Well, they've got that here. They've got a lot of that here."

Maxwell felt comfortable enough to be totally blunt. "I know that's the hype. But from what I've seen so far, what happens in Vegas is pretty weak, even by Milwaukee standards. I always thought Sin City was supposed to be some kind of modern-day Babylon. Some Babylon this is."

"Be careful what you wish for, youngblood. Particularly when it comes to those fleshly wishes. The daughters of men are fair, and even the Watchers fell. What chance do you think *you've* got?"

Maxwell came to the point. "All due respect, Reverend, but that's the whole point. I came to Las Vegas specifically *to* fall... and the harder the better... pun very much intended. Besides, in order to appreciate the glories of heaven, sometimes you need to go straight to hell."

Reverend Gator considered Maxwell's words with a look of mock astonishment. "This youngblood here is a philosopher!" Reverend Gator laughed. "I've been around, but I ain't never heard that before. That's heavy duty right there. It might be over my head."

Maxwell had some radar of his own. "Somehow I doubt that. I know a man of the world when I see one. Takes one to know one. You've been around, all right. Now, you're preaching, but back in the day you were just *reaching*—for wine, women, and song. Am I wrong?"

Reverend Gator was busted. "Nope, you're not wrong. And the list was a lot longer than that, too." He laughed at the memories.

Maxwell laughed, too. "Yeah, no doubt. I can only imagine."

Reverend Gator shook his head. "No, you can't possibly imagine. Back in the day, I was, well—balls deep in Babylon."

The trio burst into laughter.

"Did he really just say that?" Asked Curtis.

"I don't believe it," said Norby.

"And in a church, too," said Maxwell. "You've got a way with words, Reverend Gator."

The reverend's smile remained, but his eyes were serious. "You know where Babylon is, youngblood?" He tapped his temple with an index finger. "It's right here. So, you don't have to travel very far to get to it. You didn't even have to come here."

"Tell me about it," Maxwell commented. "Sorry I did."

"You're pretty dope for a preacher," said Curtis.

"Here we are in Las Vegas on a Saturday night and sitting in a church," said Norby.

Reverend Gator nodded. "But where will you be sitting in the afterlife, smoking or non-smoking."

The trio laughed.

Maxwell admired Reverend Gator. "I love your style, Reverend. Smooth, non-judgmental, no fire and brimstone. Most preachers treat the Bible like a sledgehammer, but not you. And yet you do make your point. You're like Bruce Lee, only you're doing spiritual Jeet Kune Do—the art of preaching without preaching. You're no yellow belt, that's for sure."

Reverend Gator answered, imitating Elvis Presley, "Thank you. Thank you very much."

"You'll save more souls than the average preacher, that's for sure," Maxwell added.

"But will I save yours?"

Curtis glanced at his watch. "Maybe we should start heading back now. I'm getting hungry."

The trio stood. Reverend Gator finished his music with a particularly ominous chord. He stood, stepped off the stage, and approached his guests.

"I'll walk you out."

The busy workers continued their tasks as Reverend Gator escorted the trio over to the entrance door. The men exited the church and out into the night. Reverend Gator shook the hand of each man warmly, saving Maxwell for last.

"Thanks for dropping in. I really enjoyed it."

"It was good hanging out with you, too, Reverend. I came to Vegas and ended up in church. Just what my mom would have wanted." Maxwell laughed.

"In Las Vegas, anything is possible. Who knows? The night is still young. You might just find what you're looking for."

"That's a truly scrumptious thought indeed, but it's highly unlikely. We're leaving in the morning, anyway. So, we'll just end up at another strip club. Just what I'm not looking for."

Reverend Gator eyed Maxwell up and down. He understood. "You're not just looking for flesh. You're looking for *strange* flesh."

"I like you, Reverend Gator, because you truly understand. Yeah, that's exactly what I'm looking for. Strange flesh. And the stranger, the better." Maxwell smiled as he dreamed the impossible dream. "You want to know what I want? Babylon Wood."

Reverend Gator looked surprised. "Babylon Wood? Really?" He casually pointed to the doorway of the storefront next door to his church. The establishment appeared to be closed. There was no lighting or signage, and the windows were painted black.

"That's over there."

Curtis and Norby cracked up laughing. Maxwell laughed, too, at first. But the strange look in the reverend's eyes brought his laughter to a sudden halt. Reverend Gator wasn't smiling. He wasn't kidding, either.

"What are you talking about? asked Maxwell. "That's not real."

"Babylon Wood is as real as it gets."

Curtis and Norby stopped laughing.

"Somebody told you about Babylon Wood, but they said what—it was just an urban legend? Well, whoever told you that is playing games with you. Who told you, anyway?"

"The cab driver who dropped us off," replied Maxwell.

"Yeah? Well, a lot of cab drivers know what's up. They'd better stay up with Uber and Lyft on their ass."

"But he said it was just a metaphor."

Reverend Gator motioned toward the mysterious storefront. "I got your metaphor right there. Funny how he brought you right to it, too. Small world, isn't it?" He smiled mischievously. "Damn, talk about a cosmic coincidence. What are the odds? But it's like I told you—in Las Vegas, anything is possible. Now you understand."

Maxwell didn't understand at all. "Strange flesh next door to a church?"

Reverend Gator looked at Maxwell with mock bewilderment, then shook his head with disappointment. "Come on, youngblood. I thought you were a man of the world. You're just a yellow belt." He laughed. "Welcome to the real Las Vegas. Heaven and hell sit across the street from each other. Angels and demons are next door neighbors." He tapped his temple. "Babylon is right here." He pointed to the storefront. "And strange flesh is over there."

The reverend's demeanor was distinctly different from before. Inside the church, he was a preacher, yet chill and laid back. But now, he seemed like a different person entirely. His vibe was unnerving, even chilling. His eyes were blazing. The trio stared at him, silent, and more than a bit afraid.

"You youngbloods are looking a little scared now. Are you scared? It's okay. Nothing to be ashamed of. Fear is a healthy response. It can keep you alive if you let it. You wanted the ultimate sexual experience? Well, guess what? You just found it. And it's within walking distance, too. You hit the jackpot. What were the odds?"

"What goes on in there, anyway?" Asked Norby.

"I have no idea. I was a man of the world, all right, but I never had that particular experience. I don't know what goes on in there. Ain't but one way to find out, though. Are you sure you want to? Are you ready?"

The trio looked at one another.

"Here's my suggestion. Go have some dinner, then leave this place as fast as you can. You've seen enough Vegas for one visit, anyway. Go back to your hotel and go to bed. Then check out in the morning and get your rookie yellow belt asses back to Milwaukee where you belong." He pointed toward the storefront. "Let whatever happens there stay there."

A worker opened the door of the church and peered out. "Excuse me, Reverend. I'm sorry to bother you, but could you come inside and take a look at something, please?"

"Be right there." Reverend Gator walked away from the trio and headed back toward his church. He paused at the door for a moment, then turned to offer one last word. "You can have anything you want in this world, but you have to pay for it. Sometimes, the price is high. Make sure you can afford it." Reverend Gator entered the church, leaving the trio to ponder his words.

"That old dude is trippin'," said Curtis.

Maxwell glanced over at the storefront. "Bullshit. That man is as real as it gets. If he said Babylon Wood is over there, it's over there."

"So now what?" Asked Norby.

At first, Maxwell wasn't sure. Then he considered the possibilities and had a genuine epiphany. "Maybe it's true after all."

"What are you talking about?" Asked Curtis.

"I think I just became a believer. They're right. In Las Vegas, anything is possible."

Norby looked over at the storefront. The entrance was dark, and the atmosphere was more foreboding than welcoming. "I don't know. Something feels weird."

"Yeah, it's weird, all right. We were getting ready to leave the table, and we just got dealt a winning hand. A royal flush. Royal *flesh*. Well, I'm about to play my hand right to the very end." Maxwell looked puzzled. "That cab driver—not quite sure what to make of him."

Maxwell lit a cigarette and took a long, deep drag. By the time he'd completed his exhalation, he looked enlightened, as if he'd had a genuine spiritual awakening. "Now I understand. Reverend Gator called it a cosmic coincidence. It's that, all right, but it's something else, too. What's happening tonight is sexual destiny. Cosmic sexual destiny. That's it. That's got to be it. What else could it be? Well, I'm about to go fulfill mine."

Norby wasn't so sure. "I don't know, man. I think—"

"You think what? You think we should go back to some

dumb ass strip joint for our last night in Sin City? If that's your idea of a good time, you go have a good time. Knock yourself out. By the way, there's a strip joint right here in this very complex. The cab driver told me all about it. He said it was the bomb, too." Maxwell pointed toward the storefront. "Me, I'm going over there. Babylon Wood is over there, and the hand of fate is over here, tickling my nuts."

Maxwell didn't wait for a consensus of opinion. His mind was made up. He took one last drag, then tossed his cigarette and headed for the storefront. Curtis and Norby looked at each other, unsure what to do next.

"I guess we'll eat later," said Curtis.

Curtis and Norby hurried after Maxwell, who was already at the door. Maxwell opened the door, and the trio entered a narrow, wood-paneled hallway. It was dimly lit by a single bare bulb hanging from the ceiling. At the end of the hallway was another door. The trio ventured down the hallway to the door and opened it.

They entered what appeared to be a waiting room. In contrast to the eerie exterior, the room was well lit and hospitable. The floor was hardwood, and the walls were wood paneled, like the hallway. The walls were decorated with numerous framed paintings and photographs of trees. A large wooden desk sat in the middle of the room, appearing much like the desk of a grade school teacher from yesteryear.

An elderly woman was seated at the desk. Plainly dressed and with minimum makeup, her snow-white hair was pulled back into a matronly, dignified bun. Her name was Betty, and she looked like a retired Sunday school teacher. She was talking on her cellphone.

The trio stopped dead in their tracks at the sight of her. Who is Grandma? Is this a mistake? But there was no mistake. Betty motioned for them to come in and pointed toward a wooden bench sitting against the wall directly across from her desk.

"Have a seat. I'll be right with you."

The trio exchanged confused glances, then walked over to the bench and seated themselves, with Maxwell in the middle.

"I feel like I'm in the principal's office," Maxwell said quietly.

A few feet behind Betty, Maxwell noticed a wooden door. Etched in the door was an ornate carving of a tree. It was a stunning piece of furniture that seemed out of place in the plain surroundings. Betty finally ended her conversation and placed her cellphone on the desk.

"Sorry to keep you waiting. May I help you?" Her smile was as sunny as her disposition.

The trio looked confused again, then embarrassed. Curtis and Norby looked to Maxwell for leadership.

"Uh, yes," Maxwell began. "We're looking for... we were wondering... uh." Maxwell was uncharacteristically at a loss for words. Curtis and Norby offered no assistance. Fortunately, Betty understood their unease.

"Babylon Wood?" She said with a wink.

Maxwell looked relieved. "Yes, ma'am."

"That will be one thousand dollars... each."

The trio were shocked by the price, and Curtis and Norby looked to Maxwell.

"I don't have a thousand dollars," whispered Curtis.

"Me neither," echoed Norby.

Betty opened a drawer, removed a credit card processing machine, and placed it on the desk. "We accept Visa, Mastercard, Discover, American Express, Google Plus, and PayPal."

Maxwell stood, removed his wallet, and approached the desk. He looked back at his companions, who remained seated.

"What are you waiting for?"

Curtis and Norby traded glances, then stood and joined Maxwell at the desk, albeit a bit begrudgingly. Betty processed each transaction, then returned the plastic to the owners, along with receipts. "On your statements, the charges will simply read Las Vegas Ghost Tours. I'll need your cellphones, too, please."

The trio reluctantly, but dutifully, complied. Betty placed the phones in a drawer along with a number of others. Betty stood and motioned for the trio to follow her back to the ornate door. Her sweet, grandmotherly demeanor stood in contrast to the message she delivered. Her eyes sparkled, and she grinned as if about to reveal a naughty secret.

"I'm sure you've had plenty of erections," Betty giggled. "But tonight, you nice young men are going to find out what a real hard-on is all about. *Rigidity…* on a whole new level. Believe me, you've never had anything like Babylon Wood, and you never will again. Enjoy yourselves. Goodbye."

Betty opened the door and stepped aside, allowing the trio to enter a narrow stairwell with a spiral staircase leading up. Maxwell led his companions up the stairs. At the top, they found an ornately carved door like the one below. Maxwell opened the door. A dimly lit, wood-paneled hallway stretched out before them, with a door at the end. They proceeded.

"A thousand dollars?" Norby still couldn't believe it. "We don't even know—"

"Relax. You'll get your money's worth. If there's one thing in this world I trust, it's my nuts. We're about to take a trip back in time. Back to Babylon. The most perverted, demented, sexually twisted city in human history. The real Sin City."

At the end of the hallway, the trio reached a door that was an ornate duplicate of the others. The hallway went pitch black, and the door opened. Music and color seeped out into the hallway. The color was purple, and the music was House. A woman stood before them, wearing a garment more negligee than dress. It completely covered her yet revealed everything she had to offer. The woman was stunning, but her eyes were dark and lifeless. There was no smile on her face. Her name was Tanya. She stepped aside.

The trio entered a cavernous room that looked like a purple pit. In the middle of the pit was a round dancefloor packed with dancers gyrating to the pulsing music. Onlookers sat at tables that surrounded the dancers. Comfortable lounge furniture was scattered throughout the room, as well as strategically placed pillars and statuary. The walls were draped with purple silk, and the floor was covered with ornate, Persian rugs. This room would have made a fitting orgy chamber for royal freaks from antiquity.

The chamber was filled with women. There were a dozen or so men who, like the trio, had probably found this place by chance. But this was clearly a venue for women. They came in various sizes, shapes, ages, and ethnicities. Many of them were dressed provocatively like Tanya, others more conservatively. There was a distinct vibe of camaraderie in the air, as if these women were all part of some secret society.

Maxwell hungrily eyed the sensual feast spread out before him. "This ain't Chuck E. Cheese. This is Babylon… for real. We're going to hell this evening. And it's about time, too."

Curtis agreed. "I think you might just be right for once." He laughed. "Do we really have to leave tomorrow?"

Tanya closed and locked the door behind them. "You're not going anywhere." Her voice was a whisper and went unheard.

Tanya walked away, and a waitress dressed in a top hat and tuxedo approached the trio, wheeling a cart filled with a variety of colorful drinks. Each man made his selection, and the waitress continued on her way.

Maxwell raised his goblet to make a toast. "Here's to fabulous Las Vegas, the greatest city in the whole—"

"Shut up, asshole," interrupted Curtis. "This is crazy luck, and you know it." Curtis glanced over at Norby, who had yet to offer any feedback. "What do you think?"

"It's okay."

Maxwell looked at Norby with astonishment, then annoyance. "Okay? Are you insane? Have you ever seen anything like this in Milwaukee? Or in your dreams? Dumb ass strip clubs are okay. This is nirvana on steroids. What's wrong with you? We should've dropped you off at that strip joint."

Several beautiful women, all dressed like Tanya, approached the trio. They encircled the men and inspected them. Like Tanya, they, too, had the same black orbs for eyes, but unlike Tanya, these women were smiling. They radiated a predatory sexuality, boldly rubbing their bodies against the men and flicking their tongues hungrily. They were a horndog's wet dream come true.

Maxwell and Curtis were soon flanked by women and led out to the dancefloor. A woman advanced toward Norby, but he reflexively backed away, as if repulsed. She glared at him angrily, and the look in her black eyes was frightening. Then she hissed and walked away. An unnerved Norby took refuge in the shadows behind a pillar where he had full view of the chamber.

Something was wrong with this place and with these women. Norby knew it, even if his friends did not. The women were certainly beautiful and desirable, yet they were disturbing as well. As Norby watched the proceedings from his shadowy vantage point, his apprehension only grew. From a distance, he saw Maxwell and Curtis on the dancefloor, engulfed by women. They looked like they were in heaven.

The booming House music slowly decreased in volume,

and the lighting was dimmed. A door in a far corner opened, and two men playing large hand drums appeared. They looked to be quite old with unusually long white beards. They were dressed in floor length white robes and white head wraps. Though the men were old, their drumming was strong and loud. The rhythm they played was slow, exotic, and hypnotic, probably a long-lost rhythm from ancient times. The drummers seated themselves on pillows placed at the edge of the dancefloor that had now cleared. Spectators encircled the dance floor.

An old woman emerged from the crowd. Like the drummers, she was dressed in flowing white, but her head was uncovered. Her long, thick white hair hung far down her back. The woman carried a twisted wooden wand and joined the drummers but remained standing. She raised the wand, which proved to be not a wand, but rather a strange wind instrument. She placed the instrument to her lips and played a haunting melody to accompany the rhythm. Some women in the crowd sang along with the music in some unintelligible language. The addition of the human voices only served to maximize the eerie, ethereal quality of the music, clearly of another place and time.

A young woman clad in sheer purple silk made her way onto the dance floor, crawling on her belly. Like a serpent, she twisted and slithered, then slowly and dramatically rose to her bare feet. She was gorgeous. She was also an accomplished dancer, and her movements were both sensual and acrobatic. Her name was Sadira, and she was an aphrodisiac in the flesh.

A woman brought out a stool and placed it in the middle of the dance floor. Another woman took Curtis by the hand, led him from out of the crowd of spectators, and seated him. Then she bound his wrists behind his back with a cord. Curtis didn't protest but rather smiled in anticipation of whatever experience was to follow. He was expecting an unusual lap dance. Sadira circled Curtis, moving provocatively, fueled by the growing intensity of the music. Like a shaman, she entered a trance state, induced by the rhythm of the drums.

Maxwell watched from the sidelines with an envious grin. Still hidden away in the shadows, Norby watched from across the chamber. It was a sexy sight to be sure, but he remained wary. His unease intensified when he noticed the movement high above.

The ceiling was constructed with large, parallel wood beams. Norby spotted several women seated on the beams, watching the action below. One of the women dropped a rope—and the opening of a noose fell just beside Curtis's head. Sadira snatched the noose, slipped it around Curtis's neck, and tightened it. The woman high above jumped off the wooden beam while clutching the rope. When she dropped to the floor, the force of her weight jerked the rope, causing Curtis to shoot up off the stool and into the air.

The entire chamber of women swooned in simultaneous delight and applauded. The few men in attendance looked on in horrified disbelief, none more so than Maxwell. He was paralyzed by the sight. Curtis violently struggled and spasmed as he dangled at the end of the rope, suspended several feet off the ground. His eyes bulged, and his tongue protruded from his mouth. He couldn't scream because of the choking. The woman holding the rope was easily strong enough to maintain her grip. She looked up at the dangling Curtis with a triumphant smile.

But the worst was yet to come. Two more women emerged from the onlookers. They seized the violently struggling Curtis, each one grabbing a leg, and they held him fast and firm. They yanked down his trousers and underwear causing some women to point at his groin, giggling with excitement. Sadira stood a few feet away, and she looked up at Curtis lustily. Then she sprinted and propelled herself up and into the air. With her arms and legs outstretched, she looked like a flying squirrel sailing in slow motion. She slammed full force into Curtis, and the impact was so violent, the two women holding his legs were knocked to the floor. Curtis swung back and forth, bucking wildly, as Sadira clung to him, undulating furiously.

The multitude of female onlookers looked up at the ghastly sight and squealed in orgasmic unison. Many of them were so overwhelmed with arousal, they dropped to their knees and massaged their breasts and genitals. Sadira howled with pleasure, as she fucked Curtis to death—literally.

The few men in attendance now made a desperate dash for the entrance door, but they couldn't escape. Hissing women grabbed them and dragged them kicking and screaming to the dancefloor of death. Maxwell could barely stand. The horrific sight of Curtis dying so violently before his eyes was too much for him. His knees finally buckled, but two women grabbed him before he collapsed. They hurled him out onto the dancefloor to join the other men who lay cowering in terror. Women descended on them all like hungry rats, binding their hands behind them. Nooses were dropped from above, heads were forced into them, and helpless victims were jerked up and into the air. As they frantically dangled from ropes, their trousers were snatched down, and women took turns leaping up and onto them.

The frantic struggling of the dying men inflamed the lust of the onlookers to the boiling point. After one woman satisfied herself, she fell off her victim exhausted, allowing another woman to quickly take her place. The dancefloor was filled with wild-eyed women anxiously waiting for their turn. This was an orgy chamber, after all.

The strange, otherworldly music was driving and forceful and provided an appropriate soundtrack to the horror show unfolding. Indeed, the music only served to intensify the violence. The women who clung to the dying bucked their hips to the beat.

Norby remained safely hidden behind the pillar in the shadows, unable to believe the nightmare he was witnessing. The sight of a hysterical Maxwell being hoisted up to his death ignited him to action. Norby dropped to the floor, rolled over to the wall, and scurried on his hands and knees toward the entrance door, unnoticed by anyone. He unlocked the door and eased it open.

Norby crawled out of the orgy chamber and out into the hallway. It was near dark, but he could see the door at the end. He climbed to his feet, sprinted up the hallway, and burst through the door. He ran down the stairs to the waiting room door, opened it, and rushed in. There was no sign of Betty. Norby hurried over to the desk and opened the drawer to get his cellphone. The room was empty, wasn't it?

Norby looked up and saw Betty clinging to the light fixture above the desk. She dropped down on top of him, onto his back, and dragged him to the ground. Hissing like a serpent, she straddled him and clawed at him with the energy and fury of a much younger woman. Physically overwhelmed and overpowered, Norby was no match for her. Betty stood, snatched Norby by the collar, and dragged him out of the room and into the stairwell, as he screamed for his life. Betty slammed the door closed behind her.

* * *

Reuben was cockily confident his latest tale had done the dirty deed with the expected results. Surely he'd given Jill the O face she'd been seeking. "I know I got you off with that one. You probably need a cigarette by now." Reuben laughed with stud-like assurance.

Jill's makeshift desk was again covered with detailed note cards. The notebook in her lap contained a meticulously drawn image of a hanging man being screwed by a clinging sex demon. She'd never seen anything like it. As Jill stared at the image, she did indeed have an O face.

"Well?" Reuben sounded impatient. He knew he'd delivered the goods.

Jill took a deep breath as she eased back into character and back onto the tightrope of lies. It was going to be a serious challenge. This story had proven to be her favorite by far. Her response would need to be epic.

"Reuben, you're a creative storyteller, you really are. You've proven it over and over again. I'm convinced, okay? But the problem with this story is… well… it's just plain nasty. In fact, it's the most offensive story I've ever heard in my life. And that's saying a lot. It's entirely too vulgar."

Reuben was shocked. It was hardly the response he was expecting. "Too vulgar? Are you serious? I mean, you do know what happens when a guy gets strung up by the neck, don't you?"

"Yes. I'm familiar with the physical responses."

"Well, if a Babylonian sex demon was going to do a guy, isn't that how she'd do it? Think about it. It's totally logical, in a sexually demonic sort of way. And what about the reverend? He's the angel at the crossroads. He's pivotal. On screen for five minutes and he almost steals the show. This story has got everything. It's got horror, philosophy, spirituality, even some comedy."

"And unfortunately, pornography."

"Pornography? You asked for a Vegas sex story, and I gave you one. Besides, one person's pornography is another person's afterschool special."

"That story you just told me is no afterschool special… unless you're a kid named Clive Barker."

Reuben struggled to contain his obvious frustration. "I just don't understand where you're coming from. You're Carfax Abbey. You produce horror films. You've pushed the envelope, too. I would think you'd—"

"But I never pushed it this hard or this far, that's for sure. The story you just told me is repugnant. I really don't think the general public is ready for anything so repulsive."

"Repugnant? Repulsive?" Reuben laughed cynically. "Is this a limo or the Westboro Baptist Church? I'm shocked you're shocked. I seem to remember a film… what was it called? Oh yeah, *Lesbian Vampire Reform School.* Ever hear of that one?"

That film was a sore spot best forgotten, and Jill responded defensively. "Well, for the record, Reuben, that was my first picture, and that was a long time ago. But I never produced anything that had chicks screwing cadavers hanging by the neck. That's just depraved."

Reuben fell silent.

"Reuben?"

Reuben didn't answer.

"Reuben, please don't be upset, okay? It's a very creative story, just like all your stories. But it's… well… perverted, that's all."

"Well, so is Las Vegas. Why do you think people come here, anyway? The buffets?"

A beeping noise could be heard from Reuben's side of the partition.

"Hold on, I just got a text," said Reuben. "Good news. My girl Shauntay just scored you a room at the Cosmo right on the Strip. How about that? I told you I'd hook you up. You just hit the jackpot."

Jill smiled like a reptile, as she surveyed her abundant new notes. "Nice! You did it, Reuben. Thank you so much. You really did come through for me."

"Not like I wanted to, though." Reuben sounded depressed. There was no more wind in his sails. "I didn't impress you with my stories. I know that."

"That's not true, Reuben. On the contrary, I'm more than impressed. And I'll prove it to you. As soon as I get back to L.A., I'm going to mention you to an agent friend of mine. Just because these particular stories aren't necessarily right for me doesn't mean you're not talented, because you are. I think you've got a bold, original voice that deserves to be heard. So, I'm going to do everything in my power to help you reach the right person. I give you my word."

"Really? You'd do that for me?" Reuben was excited by the prospect. "You really mean it?"

Jill turned off her cellphone, which had been recording since Reuben's first story. She placed the phone in her purse. She gathered the note cards for Reuben's latest story, secured them with rubber bands, and placed them inside her briefcase along with her sketchbook.

"Of course, I really mean it, Reuben. Honestly."

Jill would remember this night for the rest of her life. Just as Crystal, her psychic, had foretold, she had indeed hit a jackpot far beyond her wildest imaginings. She had wept about her lack of ideas, afraid that her stint in Hollywood had left her creatively bankrupt. Now she was ready to weep for joy. Now she had far more than ideas. Her briefcase was filled with *magic*, and she stroked it lovingly. Inside her briefcase was everything she needed to rejuvenate her career, and more importantly, totally reinvent herself. Now she had the tools. Tonight was more than a jackpot; it was a dream come true. It was unbelievable.

Jill's work was done. Now she could relax again. She returned to the seat opposite the dividing partition and removed her pipe from her purse. She took a long, deep hit, but as she exhaled, she was suddenly seized by a terrifying thought.

"Uh, Reuben, I was just wondering something. Have you registered these stories with the Library of Congress?"

"The Library of Congress? No, I hadn't even thought about it. They're safe and sound inside my laptop. But now that you mention it, maybe I should."

"Don't worry about it." Jill looked relieved and relaxed again. "I'll take care of it. Just send me everything you've got, and I'll get it all registered for you in your name. After everything you've done for me, it's the least I can do for you."

"Really? Wow, that would be great."

"It's my pleasure. Regardless of whatever misgivings I had about your stories, I think you're an amazing writer. You're a story brat. That's for sure."

"Thank you. That means a lot coming from someone like you."

"Well, I really mean it. Honestly."

"My dream came true tonight. I always wanted to pitch my ideas to Hollywood, and tonight I got my chance. This is a night I won't ever forget, that's for sure."

Jill sat back in her seat and took another hit. She exhaled, without remorse. "Likewise."

"I was wondering if you could do one more thing for me?"

"Anything, Reuben. What do you want me to do?"

"Smile for the cameras."

Jill snapped to an upright position. Her eyes darted around the interior of the limo, searching for hidden devices. She didn't see them, but she knew she was busted. She looked as though she'd swallowed a knife.

"This is Vegas, girlfriend. Cameras are everywhere, including back there. Gotta be careful who you pick up these days. You could end up getting robbed if you're not careful. You're very thorough. Did you get everything on those note cards?" Reuben's tone was ice cold.

Jill panicked. "Reuben, I know how this must look. But it's not what you think. Honestly. I swear. I always take little notes like that. It's just a professional habit I've got. That's all."

"You draw very well, by the way."

"Those little doodles? I do that, too. Just another professional habit. It doesn't mean anything. Honestly."

"You might want to check the battery on your cellphone. It was on for a while."

The limo jerked to a sudden dead stop. The mesh grille built into the dividing partition was ripped away. Reuben pressed his face into the opening. It was the face of rage."

"You stole my work!" Reuben screamed.

"Honestly, Reuben, it's not what you think! You've got it all wrong! I would never steal—"

Reuben's head pushed completely through the opening,

and Jill screamed in horror. Reuben was not human. He was a serpentine creature with a human head attached to a thick, snake-like body. His lower half remained behind the dividing partition while the rest of him extended out through the opening, bobbing and weaving like a cobra ready to strike.

Jill screamed. "Oh, my God! This can't be happening!"

Reuben's head swelled, and his mouth widened, revealing a large, full set of teeth. Jill screamed for the last time. Reuben lunged at her and swallowed her head completely. Jill flailed and thrashed in a futile attempt to free herself from Reuben's jaws. She looked like a ragdoll in the mouth of a beast. Reuben slammed her into the rear back window, shattering it to pieces. He bit Jill's head off completely and pushed her spasming body out through the open window. Finally, he spit out her head like a piece of chewing gum. The limo drove away, moving down the alley as if in slow motion.

Jill's headless, quivering body lay sprawled on the ground. Her head lay a few feet away. Though decapitated, she was still quite conscious. Her bulging eyes watched as her body twitched and convulsed reflexively. Her mouth moved as if she wanted to scream. As the light of her life slowly dimmed, Jill then realized the horrifying truth of Reuben's words. He'd been right all along.

In Wack City, anything is possible.

About the Author

Miko Montgomery is a writer, musician/composer, photographer and filmmaker.

mikomontgomery.com